The Mythicia Chronicles

Book 1: The Destined

By Joseph Russell

For Chris,

Hope you enjoy it!

All the best,

Joseph Russell

Cover Art by Kaan Vardal

ISBN-10: 978-1481173056
ISBN-13: 978-1481173056

For you

Prologue

Malcaractimus slowly rose from his demonic throne. His architects had crafted it from the bones of his enemies. There had been more than enough bones to build it, and even more enemies to replenish it if it were ever in need of repair. Some of its contributors were the previous government, before he rose to power. Some were of the united army, whom he had conquered. And some were rebels.

Rebels - the plague of his empire, the last wretched mortals who dared to oppose him. No number of defeats seemed to be able to deter that damnable terrorist Prometheus, self-styled leader of the resistance, from harassing his forces at every turn. The resistance was like an itch, and no matter how much he scratched it, it refused to subside. But soon that would not matter. In two orbits of Lunadraxis 5, the Black Star would rise, the prophecy would be fulfilled, and he would crush the resistance once and for all. It was ironic to think that the last hope of the very rebels who defied him would soon become his greatest weapon.

The demon-emperor Malcaractimus laughed quietly to himself as he strode towards the glinting gunmetal doors that led out of his throne room and into the main part of his fortress. He breathed deeply, basking in the delightful odour that rose from the kitchens below. They would, of course, be preparing elf meat. Who could have thought that the creatures that formed the backbone of the resistance could be so... delectable? He placed a claw on a thin green pane of glass embedded into a wall, and the doors slid silently open.

He padded into the room, smiling as he beheld the results of the work that had taken him over a hundred years to complete. He stood in a great circular dome of smooth, uninterrupted silver, the floors lined with crumpled plastic sheeting. But what lay in the centre of the dome was his true victory – his pride and joy. To an untrained eye, what he beheld were but slabs of polished black stone, positioned in a perfect circle. But to Malcaractimus, it was so much more. This circle had once been a monolith gate, a dormant portal that could take a being to another identical circle in the universe. Now though, thanks to Malcaractimus' efforts, it could be the key to becoming a god.

The emperor's dreaming was interrupted, however, by one of his multitude of slaves. The monolith gate was of utmost importance, and had to be preserved until the prophecy came about. The slave in question had been in the process of carrying preservation fluid between the stones, and in his haste had failed to look where exactly he was going. He had not seen the emperor enter the room, and stumbled right into his muscle-knotted chest. Malcaractimus glared at the pitiful creature that cowered before him. *A runt*, he observed. It was unusual for runts to achieve the personal service of the Emperor. Still, that made him all the more... expendable.

The slave's eyes widened as he stared up at the ruler of all he had ever known. His mouth moved silently for several seconds, and then at last a few words trickled forth. "I'm sorry, lord!" the slave managed to whimper. "I give you my word that it'll never happen again! I'll try and make it up to you, I swear I will."

"And how," the demon replied, unsheathing his claws, "Will you do so from beyond the grave?"

"What?" gasped the slave, the trickling stream of words dammed by the malice blazing from the emperor's every word.

"I haven't eaten since breakfast. Now, I know I'm scheduled for a feast in an hour, but I'm sure it wouldn't be rude to take my starter... early."

Malcaractimus grinned, and started his meal.

Nicholas the Wise typed feverishly into his computer. "Come on, come on come on come on..." he muttered to himself. He stopped and glanced up at the screen. With a long and work-strained groan, the monitor flickered, and settled at a miserable blue.

"Thaumaturgical levels at zero. No match detected," the computer stated in a female monotone.

"Damn!" the mage cursed, swivelling away and flicking on his coffee machine. He stared bleakly at the cramped office in which he worked. Plain whitewashed walls, a simple desk, a smart F3000 Hypercomputer and an old Earth Delonghi Espresso maker stared back at him. One would have thought that with the resources the Rebel Alliance had to hand, they could have supplied him with a decent workspace, but it wasn't worth complaining. He'd only be sent dodgy coffee as well.

Three sharp raps on the door penetrated Nick's silent mournfulness.

"Come in!" Nick called.

A tall teenage boy with long blonde hair, blue eyes, and a budding civilization of acne closed the door behind him. "Any luck, master?" he asked.

"Sorry, Alex," Nick replied, shaking his head. "I really thought I had it this time. Any word from General Boar? How is it at the front?"

Alex sighed. "It's not good, master. Malcaractimus' forces grow stronger by the day. They've nearly taken Garactoid."

Nick sadly sipped his coffee. “We haven’t got much hope then. I’ve been studying the prophecy. “The Destined” is predicted to appear within the week. I’ve been scanning for any thaumaturgical energy spikes on Earth, but there’s nothing. If anything, it’s abnormally *low*. It’s a shame we didn’t have longer at the school – it would have been so much easier there.”

“Master, the gate was closing. You know we couldn’t have remained there any longer. We were lucky to get the chance we did – not everyone stumbles across Mythicia’s last link to Earth. You know there’s only enough Imaginarium for one more trip, and we can’t do that unless we find the Destined from here.” Alex said. “This is a prophecy we’re talking about. You yourself said fate works in funny ways. Maybe there won’t be a spike from the Destined. Maybe his powers won’t awaken until the week has passed.”

“Yes, you could be right, Alex, but we can’t afford to wait that long. Malcaractimus is working on something big, we know he is. Time is running out, and we need the Destined *now*. But how are we supposed to trace magic that doesn’t exist yet?”

Alex was silent for a moment. “Couldn’t we use a Hiladfagh Malicotatem incantation on the Imaginarium itself? Any substance that can cross to a universe where time runs more slowly has to cross time itself. The spell could follow the energy transfer, and give us a reading from a week in the future.”

Nick considered the possibility. “It’s worth a try,” he concluded. Alex threw a mock salute, and grinning, darted out of the room. It really was fascinating to see Alex’s mind at work. The magnificent ideas were one of the reasons he kept the boy around. After a moment’s pause, the boy returned with a jagged, glittering fragment of crystal nestled in the palm of his hand. Looking at the stone, the colours seemed to shift; one moment it seemed almost red, and then, *without undergoing any apparent change*, it was a sort of blueish-green. The next moment it was a pure white, and then midnight black. To a newcomer, it would have been captivating. But neither mage nor apprentice so much as glanced at the stone. More important matters were at hand.

Alex handed it to Nick, who inserted it into an indent in the side of the computer. The machine beeped, and the female monotone of the computer intoned: "Focus object accepted. Scanning."

As the machine whirred, the mage murmured a multitude of barely pronounceable words under his breath. Alex leaned over Nick's shoulder whilst the mage tapped away furiously. They both stared at the screen.

In a far corner of the screen, a green light flickered faintly. The computer's synthesised voice said: "Match detected."

The two men leapt to their feet, their hands meeting in a powerful hi-five.

"Yes!" Nick whooped. "Go get him, Alex. Computer, identify."

Alex stood up, but stopped. A name had appeared on the screen.

"No..." breathed Nick. "To think we knew him all that time..."

"And we never realised..." murmured Alex.

As Alex turned and hurtled out of the room, something changed across Mythicia. Even the smallest of life forms could sense it. Something was coming.

In the city of Atlantis, centrepiece of the resistance, King Prometheus raised his head.

In the underground caverns of Panoga, a goblin slid into unconsciousness.

In the ruined city of Odmehlwor, a guard demon dropped his sword.

In the Iron Fortress of the Bull Lord's kingdom, the Minotaur Council called an emergency meeting.

In the endless night of Hades IV, a necromancer fumbled an incantation.

And in another universe, in the darkest bowels of a scorched hill, something stirred...

Chapter 1

4:15

Thomas Colfrey was the boy with no friends. It wasn't that he didn't enjoy being with other people, it was just that until recently, he hadn't needed to spend time with many other people. He'd always been one of those people who have one or two really good friends, and the rest are just acquaintances. Not the sort of person who somehow manages to be friends with *everyone*. He couldn't stand those people.

And that had been all right. His best friend was never ill, never off school, not ever. So he always had someone to depend upon for company. The point where the system stopped working, however, was if said friend just... went.

It had been a whole year since Nick had vanished. They had been in a lesson, and Nick had put up his hand and asked to go to the toilet. He had left the room, but never came back.

If that wasn't weird enough, at exactly that moment, Nick's younger brother Alex had gone as well. They had both disappeared without a trace.

Nobody had known where they had gone. They had simply vanished off the face of the Earth. People had looked for them; there had been a search of the school, police investigations, and even T.V. appeals for the children to come home. But they never did. Never, ever, ever.

Sometimes Thomas wondered what had really happened. Had the brothers been abducted? Kidnapped? You heard about that happening on the news all the time: children disappearing, being smuggled off to some foreign country to be used as slaves, or even just being taken away to some dank room in Britain before being abused and killed. But somehow, he didn't think that was the case. Nick wasn't stupid enough just to go off with a stranger, although of course, Thomas supposed, he could have been taken by force. Perhaps.

The strangest thing was, though, there had been nothing from their parents. The police had gone to No. 40 Englefield Road - the address registered under Nicholas Henson at school, but they came up with nothing. There was no No. 40. The road ended at 39. There was no house there, and no one nearby had any recollection of there ever being a No. 40.

Miserably, Thomas scuffed his way along the tennis court tram lines, just as he had done, it seemed, a hundred times before. A shaft of sunlight lanced off a football as it rolled across his path. He absentmindedly nudged the thing aside. The sun beamed down across the quad, the concrete rectangle where everyone went at break times. Hah, in different circumstances, and with exams coming up, the good weather could almost have been called auspicious. But now it was just like God was rubbing all the good of the world in his face. He had been leading a perfectly normal, happy life, until his best friend had just upped and gone, without saying a word.

The shrill ring of the end of break bell sliced through his thoughts like a knife. Thomas headed for the Science lab. Of course, the school had invested thousands of pounds in its Science block, and everything was typically state of the art. Gas piping, iPads, interactive whiteboards, it had the lot. Education seemed to be top of the list on the new Prime Minister's agenda – he'd invested millions in technology for schools all across Britain. He'd even turned up at Thomas' school to open the new Science block, although he'd been off with chicken pox that day – just his luck.

It was an intensely boring Science lesson. Dr Hedge was rambling on about particle accelerators and antimatter, somehow culminating in a speech about the mystery of the animals of the deep, but Thomas couldn't care less. He studied the poster about an upside-down rainbow on the wall.

"Colfrey!" barked Hedge, his caterpillar eyebrows writhing with indignation. "Why precisely does the blobfish appear to have a human nose?"

Thomas froze. Dr Hedge had just asked him a question. Desperately, he cast his eyes around the room, searching for any form of inspiration, but under the combined gaze of all of his class, he had no hope. He gave in.

"I'm sorry sir?" he asked feebly.

"You *were* listening, weren't you?" Hedge asked menacingly.

"Err... Absolutely, sir!"

"Detention, my office, 12:30!" bellowed Hedge. "From now on, listen when I talk to you! Get it?"

"Got it."

"Good."

Thomas left Science an hour later. It was lunch break; that meant he had twenty minutes to eat till he was expected for detention. His mother would be disappointed, he knew, but there was nothing he could do about it. Trying to talk your way around Dr Hedge was like trying to knock down a mountain with a damp sponge.

Hurrying into the canteen, Thomas shuffled up to the food counter. An unsmiling dinner lady pushed a steaming bowl of stew into his outstretched hands, and he suppressed a wince as he realised hot food meant hot bowls as well. As he turned to look for a seat, he moaned with dismay as his gaze fell upon one at the end of the furthest table from him. Raiza's table.

Raiza was the school bully, and also Thomas' no. 1 worst enemy. He was a moderately tall, ratty boy, brilliant at football, and strangely enough, not that bad at the academic subjects either. Thomas *hated* that. He didn't see how a boy could be popular *and* clever at the same time.

It never made sense. It was always the people who were the most despicable who somehow were the most popular. A perfectly nice, genial guy could spend a day without even being glanced at by a girl, and yet one who was belittling and sadistic seemed to be surrounded by... practically everyone.

As soon as the bully saw Thomas, he grinned his malicious grin, and called him over. Thomas frantically glanced around for another option, but of course, there was none. In a feat of desperation, he made for the door, but Raiza's henchmen, Lump and Boil, reared up like two bull elephants to block his way. The brothers didn't protest about the nicknames Raiza had given them. In fact, they didn't protest about anything Raiza did. He could probably convince them that the sky was green without a word of argument. They weren't very good with words consisting of more than two syllables.

Lump managed to line his three brain cells up, and grunted: "Da boss wants a word wid you." Boil clearly felt intimidated by his brother's achievement, and so added on the words: "Yeah. Wad he said," his eyebrows meeting at his forehead with the immense concentration required to string four words together. Nevertheless, Thomas' heart sank as they marched him over to Raiza's table, and pushed him into the empty seat. Raiza smiled.

"Had fun in Science, did you?" he asked, sarcasm dripping from his every word. "We *all* agreed that Science simply wasn't good enough for someone as high and mighty as *you*. In fact, we were *so* sorry for you that we decided to cheer you up. Here."

Raiza handed Thomas an envelope.

"Go on, open it."

Thomas stared at it for a few seconds. What was he meant to do? On one hand, it could be some sort of prank designed to make Thomas look like an idiot, or it could have something in it meant to disgust him. It certainly wasn't an apology for all the times Raiza had made Thomas feel wretched. But no, if he didn't open it, he would be called a wimp, and bullied all the more. Thomas steeled himself, and opened the envelope. Inside was a small, folded card that read:

You are invited to Raiza's **party!**

Where: Behind the old bike shed

When: 4:15 today.

See you there!

"I'm sure you're very grateful, but there's no need to thank us! Anything for a nerd in need!" Raiza laughed his horrible, hyena-like laugh. At that moment, another boy got up from his seat across the lunch hall. His heart throbbing with relief, Thomas snatched up his stew and half-ran towards the vacant space. He flopped into the seat, relief radiating from his every pore.

A slim, dark haired girl leaving the lunch queue caught his eye. Whilst she wore the same uniform as the rest of the school, she was somehow glamorous in it, glowing with pride and beauty. It was

Samantha, Raiza's girlfriend. Thomas' mind span when he saw her, and his chest tightened as he was suddenly aware of how pathetic he looked. Her deep brown eyes met his, and he looked away sharply, blood rushing to his cheeks. She walked over to Raiza's table, and, with the air of someone who is about to do something she had never wanted to even dream of, she tentatively sat down. Samantha turned and glanced apologetically and pityingly at Thomas, then rotated back round to listen to Raiza's boasts. Thomas gazed dreamily after her. Some boys would describe her as "the hottest girl this side of London." Thomas most certainly agreed with them.

He finished his stew then headed towards the door. As he walked by Raiza's table, Raiza called to him.

"See you later, nerd!"

Thomas flushed again and headed almost gratefully to detention. At least no one would bother him there. "Ah, Mr Colfrey," Hedge said almost cheerfully as Thomas closed the door behind him. "I'm glad you had the presence of mind to join me. Today, Mr Colfrey, you're going to be writing an essay for me. One thousand words on the merits of listening to every word your tutor says."

Thomas nodded, glumly, and took a piece of paper to his desk. Almost absent-mindedly, he scrawled line after line onto the page; afterwards he could never remember a word he'd written. All he could think about was Raiza's message, and what the Hell he was supposed to do.

Dr Hedge paced up and down the front of the classroom, ranting and waving his hands as he expressed just how disappointed he was with him and the other students in detention, and how he hoped the work they were about to do would change their ways. As he turned and strutted to his desk, one of the line-writers tossed a crumpled ball of paper at the indignant teacher, and he squawked as the projectile struck the back of his head with a satisfying "thunk".

Hedge whirled round just as Thomas was suppressing a snigger, and his eyes settled upon him. Thomas jammed a hand over his mouth, but too late; the doctor strode down towards him, his mouth curved into a snarl. Thomas' heart leapt up into his mouth, and he began to sweat, as Hedge bent down so that his nicotine-flecked teeth were but an inch away from Thomas' ear. "There are many, many ways, boy" Hedge whispered menacingly, "that I can make your days at this school a living Hell." He straightened up again, and returned to his desk. At this point, Thomas realised he had been holding his breath, and sucked in a lungful of air and relief.

The rest of the detention dragged by, and Thomas spent the rest of the day wondering what he was going to do about the invitation. He had to go, didn't he? Otherwise he'd just get more stick from Raiza. As if what he already got wasn't enough.

Finally, the bell sounded. Thomas stepped out of the last lesson of the day and stood thoughtfully as the hundreds of children that went to the school with him swarmed towards their various means of getting home. They all had different things on their minds, he knew, but he was sure that only he was worrying about what would happen behind the bike shed at 4:15. Thomas pulled himself together, and headed determinedly for across the quad. He was going to confront Raiza on his own terms, and no one was going to stop him.

The bike shed was a positioned on the far side of the school field, and so was rarely visited by anyone. Up until a couple of years ago, everyone who rode a bike had left theirs there, but since the new, more modern bike racks had been set up at the front of the school, no one bothered to take the journey up to the shed. Now it was used as a venue for anything "dodgy" that went on during and after school hours, well away from prying eyes.

By the time he had reached the flaking green building, his confidence had deserted him. Filled with dread, he cautiously poked his head round the back.

No one was there. He smiled, and stepped forward out into the battered clearing behind the shed. With an uncertain laugh, he let relief flood his heart and turned to head back to the main part of the school.

Something hard and heavy hit him across the back of his head, and his knees buckled from underneath him. He clutched his throbbing skull as Lump towered over him, his huge body blotting out the sun like a strange misshapen eclipse. Boil ripped his blazer away from him and tossed it to Raiza, who was watching with malevolent glee from his tree.

Lump was holding a cricket bat. He'd probably never played cricket in his life, and must have stolen it from someone, but if he had been capable of learning the rules, he would have made a mean batsman. He swung it down again, this time striking Thomas' kneecaps. Raiza cackled from his tree, and started sifting through the blazer's pockets. Flames of pain seared Thomas' legs, and he knew that now there was no way he could get home in one piece.

"Well, well, well…" Raiza said, his eyebrows raised with mock interest. "What have we here?" He pulled Thomas' mobile phone from a pocket, and flourished it in the air with dramatic grace. "And who has the little nerd been chatting to now?"

The phone buzzed in Raiza's hand, and a merry little tune filled the air. A name skimmed across the phone, and Raiza's eye widened with rage and disbelief. "Samantha?" he spat, leaping from the tree to land in a crouch on the ground.

"Now why," the boy said, striding towards Thomas' crumpled form, "Is *my girlfriend* calling a little roach like you?"

Thomas gulped, and pressed his face into the grass, wishing he could make himself invisible.

"I asked you a question, nerd!" Raiza clicked his fingers and Boil's foot connected sharply with Thomas' nose. With a sickening crunch, another fountain of white-hot pain erupted behind Thomas' eyes, and he writhed on the grass like a worm out of the earth.

It had been the week before that Thomas had been just leaving the library when the soft voice of Raiza's girlfriend had called his name. Thomas remembered his spine tingling as he had turned to see Samantha standing a few metres behind holding a thick textbook between her manicured fingers.

"You left this behind," she said with a smile.

Thomas' brain took a moment to register the words, stunned as it always was whenever she appeared. He smiled nervously, taking the book with fumbling fingers. His hands brushed hers, and he must have blushed, as Samantha laughed gently. "No need to be so embarrassed, Thomas," she said, shaking her head. "Raiza isn't here."

She laughed again. "You know, I don't think he's ever actually been in a library. He's so thick he probably can't even read." Her eyes twinkled, and Thomas couldn't help but smile back. But then something crossed his mind. "But you're going out with him..." he said, confused. "I wouldn't have thought you'd say something like that."

She sighed. "I'm going to break up with him soon. He's really horrible, and I've had enough of him. Here," she said, offering him a scrap of paper. Thomas took it, and saw a number written in purple pen. "Call me," she said, and then she was gone. Thomas stared open mouthed after her, and then slowly, like a tsunami building from within, jubilation and ecstasy had bubbled up inside of him. It had lasted a full day, and Thomas had entered the number into his contacts, but after the joy had died, he hadn't had the courage to call.

"She- she gave it to me," Thomas yelped. Raiza's eyes narrowed to serpentine slits, and he set the phone to loudspeaker. Then, he hit the receive call button, and all four of the boys heard Samantha's clear voice echo out behind the bike shed. "Hey, Thomas?" she said. Raiza held a finger to his lips, his eyes broadcasting a *"speak and I'll kill you"* warning. "I just wanted to ask if you were free Friday night," Samantha continued. "Maybe see a movie or something? Raiza doesn't have to know, don't worry about it."

Raiza hissed through his clenched teeth. He pressed his mouth to the phone. "He already does," the bully said. "You'll pay for this, you ungrateful little-." He dropped the phone, and crushed it beneath his heel. Looking up, he gestured, and Lump hoisted Thomas up so his head hung just inches in front of Raiza's. The bully lifted a hand and slapped him hard across the face, and then spat at Thomas right between the eyes.

Then he turned, and started to walk away. "Do what you want with him," Raiza said, leaving the clearing. "Just know that I don't want to see him in school tomorrow. Or next week for that matter. In fact, make it a month."

Lump grinned, and tossed the dangling Thomas to Boil, who turned him upside down and whirled him around by his ankle. Thomas screamed as the blood rushed into his head, grey mist creeping across the edge of his vision. Then, suddenly he was rolling over and over across the ground, crashing into a tree with a mind-splitting thud. He lay there, dazed, his sluggish mind creeping to a halt in a world now composed only of pain. His nose had to be broken, and it felt like both his kneecaps were too. He curled into a tight ball, bracing himself against the next attack, waiting for the agony. It didn't come. Through some superhuman effort, he looked up to see Boil standing bemused as a tall, blonde boy two or three years older than Thomas held Lump a foot in the air by the scruff of his neck. The blonde boy hurled him against the shed, and watched as the behemoth slid down the corrugated metal and crumpled into a heap on the floor. The he turned his gaze on Boil, who whimpered.

The boy's fist powered into Boil's stomach, the larger boy's eyes crossing comically as he too folded up. Then the stranger strode over to Thomas and placed a gentle hand on his shoulder.

Thomas looked up at his rescuer, intrigue and wonder bubbling into his mind. The boy's face was older by a few years, now about sixteen, the hair longer and uncut and the eyes deeper with a strange wisdom that enters those who have stared death in the face. But if Thomas ignored those details and looked harder, the boy was still unmistakably…

"Alex?" Thomas asked.

The boy nodded. "That's right."

"What?" Thomas murmured, staring at Nick's brother, confusion etched across his face. "How?"

"It doesn't matter," Alex replied. "I just need you to come with me."

Thomas was dumbfounded. "Where are we going?"

"Just take my hand."

Thomas bemusedly took the blonde boy's hand. Alex looked at his ruined face for a moment and cursed. "I was too late, wasn't I?" he asked.

"It's nothing," Thomas insisted, but was horribly aware of the blood dripping down from his chin. Alex placed his free hand on Thomas' cheek, and he whispered something strange and alien under his breath. Thomas gasped as he felt his nose click unaided back into its position and started as he sensed the bone knit back together. His knees crackled under immense and sourceless pressure before suddenly he found he could move both legs with ease. As the pain vanished, he scrambled to his feet. "How did you do that?" Thomas asked.

Alex ignored him, and muttered further words in an incomprehensible tongue. Reality bent, and impossibly, a strange, circular purple disc shimmered into view in front of him. It writhed and twisted before Thomas' vision, a whirling maelstrom of colour drawing him in, deeper and deeper...

"This way," Alex said, yanking Thomas' mind back into reality.

Before Thomas could protest, Alex locked his fingers around Thomas' wrist and pulled him forward. Thomas opened his mouth to ask what was supposed to be going on, but was silenced as Alex pushed him into the disc, and then he was falling, down and down into nothingness.

Thomas lived at No. 23 Click Road. It was the sort of street where everyone knew everyone else, and Thomas liked it there. He lived with his parents and his twin sister, Opal. Apparently, most people found their sisters annoying, but Thomas and Opal got along fine. He couldn't remember the last time they'd argued. Opal loved animals, and was the type of person who'd protest against putting slug-bait down in the garden. But she worried about Thomas. She knew about Nick's disappearance, and noticed how no other children ever visited the house. She pitied her brother.

That evening, Opal was more worried than ever. Every day, she took the bus home from school with Thomas, but for some reason today he hadn't turned up. Despite her protests, the bus had left without him. *He must have a club or something*, she told herself, but even then she was uneasy.

On the way home, she texted him just to be safe. "Where r u?" She was sure he'd reply as soon as he could.

When she got home, she asked her mother, who had no idea where Thomas was either. Lisa Colfrey was a wonderful mother, and always made sure she knew exactly where her children were all the time. Today, she was at a loss.

Lisa picked up a phone, and dialled Thomas' number. A vaguely female automated voice crackled back through the speaker. "The number you are calling has not been recognized," the voice said, annoyingly smooth and almost cheerful about it.

Keep calm¸ she told herself. *There's bound to be an explanation.* Slowly and carefully, she typed the number in again. The same message arrived in response. "The number you are calling has not been recognized." She slapped the receiver back down and stared at the number pad. Using one finger, she typed it in one more time. "The number you are calling as not been recognized." Lisa screeched in frustration, slamming the thing against the wall. "Of course it's recognized, it's my son's number!" she yelled. "My son's number..." She called Thomas' father, who worked as a doctor, and was still in the clinic.

After Lisa had explained the situation, through sobs of fear and anxiety. John Colfrey was equally worried. "Phone the school, dear," he advised, feigning calmness, despite his inner feelings.

She rang Thomas' school, and an unhelpful, bored-sounding secretary picked up the phone. Lisa asked about Thomas, and was told he wasn't at school.

She hung up.

After that, she phoned the police.

Chapter 2

A Whole New World

Thomas swam through the blackness. Or rather, *didn't* swim through the blackness. He wasn't sure. His entire consciousness seemed somehow uncertain; he couldn't remember where, who or what he was. Something was pulling at him, tugging him in a direction that wasn't a direction. Another something was pulling him in the opposite of that non-existent direction. He felt a queer feeling on the edge of his mind that seemed to be telling him he should be in pain. He gave into the sensation, and the agony shot him through the darkness.

A white light blasted through the blackness, and Thomas' eyes blinked open. He found himself staring into a middle aged, craggy face. Deep lines were etched into the cheeks and the grey eyes held an air of some ancient tiredness, like those of a man who has seen too much of this life.

"Hello, Thomas," the face said, creasing into a warm smile.

"Who are you?" Thomas murmured sleepily.

"Good Lord, have I changed that much?" the face replied, startled. "Well, I suppose fifty years can do that to you. Still, isn't there *anything* about me that seems familiar?"

Thomas tried to think what the thin, scraggly old man had to do with his life, but his brain didn't seem to be able to work. Everything was disorientated; he struggled to breathe. He felt unconsciousness begin to tug at him again, and let himself sink back into sleep's embrace...

"No, no, no, don't go back to sleep!" The man shook him roughly,

"Stay with me Thomas! You know me." The man turned away to look at someone in the corner of Thomas' vision. He tried to roll his eyes to look, but the energy just didn't come. "Get me two mark seven travel pills," he ordered. Thomas' confused ears became dimly aware of the sound of shuffling papers and the banging of opening and closing drawers. The older man turned back to face Thomas. "Focus!" he commanded. "I'm Nicholas Henson. Remember? I'm Nick... Nick!"

Thomas resisted the waves of nausea pulling at his mind. Nick... Could it be? Wait... he had seen Alex, so could Nick be here too? He was too tired to think about it. He'd work it out later, but for now, he just had to sleep...

"Come on, stay with me! Please, Thomas! Speak to me!" The old man shook him again. A hand offered the man two red, oval shaped pills, and he pressed them between Thomas' lips. "Swallow!" he commanded, and Thomas' groggy mind obediently swallowed.

The sour taste of the pills jolted him awake, and he suddenly recognised the old man. He hadn't seen him for a year, but it had to be...

"Nick! Is it you?" he asked.

The man nodded furiously, a broad grin spreading across his face. But how could the boy he knew such a long year ago be here? And how could he be so old? Nothing made sense here, wherever here was. Perhaps he was dreaming. But all the same, it didn't *feel* like a dream.

"What happened to you?" Thomas asked. If this were a dream, he may as well go along with it. "Where am I?"

"Rebel base 124." replied Nick, "Zone 47, planet Arcfied, GC 6136, 2136, 4786. Mythicia. As for what happened to me, well... let's just say I've been here a *long* time."

"I'm sorry; I lost you at "rebel." Mythicia? Isn't that near Dover? And you were at St. Mark's a year ago. No offence, but one year can't age someone *that* much."

Thomas stood up, and looked past Nick to the space around him. He was in a small room with shiny, grey, metallic walls. The cold metal seemed to hold a certain homeliness, and the flickering log fire built into a side only reinforced that feeling. There was a funny sort of computer in one corner, and some bunks opposite it. Typing away at the computer was Thomas' tall blonde rescuer, Alex.

"Right," began Nick, sighing gently. "I don't really know how to tell you this, but you're a long, long way from Dover. You're not even on the same planet. You're not even in the same universe."

"Good, good," said Thomas, nodding and smiling. This sort of thing happened in dreams a lot.

"Please don't interrupt. It's better if I just tell you the truth, and you can make of it what you will at the end. Look, I'll see if I can explain. Mythicia is the name we give to the universe you and I now inhabit. It is not your native universe – it is not a universe in which humanity has ever been witnessed. This universe is populated by what you know as "mythical creatures." Minotaurs, mermaids, gorgons, sphinges, all that sort of thing."

Nick stopped, as Thomas had raised both a hand and an eyebrow. "Sphinges?" the boy asked.

"Plural of sphinx," Nick explained. "Regardless, to them, *humans* are mythical. Our children are told stories of you and your world, but no one has ever known men actually existed. I can't explain *why* your race tells stories of us, and why we tell stories of you – the peoples of the two universes have never met. But I assure you now that this is *not* a mick-take, a dream, a computer simulation, a video game, or any other of the theories you've come up with whilst I've been talking. This is real."

Thomas stared at Nick for a long moment. After a while, he nodded slowly. “Go on,” he said.

“All right,” Nick replied, suddenly perplexed as to why Thomas wasn’t questioning him. And then he saw that the boy was just humouring him, utterly disbelieving his every word but not bothering to contradict him. All the same, Nick had no choice but to continue. “Now we come to the darker part. The problem of the demons. Have you heard of demons, Thomas?”

Thomas nodded. “Big red horned things that live in Hell?”

“Close enough. Well, they’re not always big, they’re rarely red, some have horns and gods know what else, and the place they live in is not exactly Hell, but other than that, full marks. Anyway, they exist as well. In fact, they happen to run this universe.”

Thomas was still groggy and confused, but even to his bleary brain this didn’t exactly sound like a good thing.

“Roughly five hundred years ago, the demons came from whatever god-forsaken place they crawl out of and invaded Mythicia. We were entirely unprepared; we had no idea what they were, it took us at least three days to work out how to kill the blighters. They took the universe by storm, and the United Races warred with them for a hundred years. And then, somehow, the demon emperor disappeared. Leaderless, the demons scattered and were defeated, and peace returned to the cosmos. But the demons are still in this universe today. They remain as crazed, evil creatures, wanting nothing more than to kill. About fifty years ago, though, a greater demon known as Malcaractimus appeared from nowhere, and within a week, the entire universe was locked in battle with a new demon army.

“But Malcaractimus was too strong. He took planet after planet – even the greatest stronghold in the universe, Mythicia’s capital, Odmehlwor was taken. The population of Mythicia was split into those who fought, and those who were killed or enslaved by Malcaractimus’

Empire. And there he sits in his Throne of Bones in the fortress that once we people called home.

"We are the last of the fighters, Mythicia's final hope. The Rebel Alliance. And, as unlikely as it might seem, only you can help us."

"Right." replied Thomas. "Frankly, I can't believe a word of this. Demons? Pull the other one; it's got bells on. But I'll go along with what you're saying, because I don't really have a choice, do I? I'll wake up in a minute anyway, so let me get this straight before I do. Demons have taken over this universe and you need me to stop them."

"That's about it," said Alex.

"Okay then," began Thomas, his head spinning. "Here's the big question. Why me?"

"Because, only certain humans are any use against demons." Nick explained. "You need a certain kind of magic. Magic only works in Mythicia, but people on Earth still have it. They just can't use it. You have magic much stronger than normal humans. So strong, in fact, that you might help turn the tide of the war."

"Magic. Right. Sure. Magic exists. So, show me some."

Nick sighed. "Lhigbort," he murmured.

He cupped his hands, and the light radiating from the lamps on the ceiling dimmed, seeming to drain away into the air. It swirled through the room, dancing and twisting before gathering in a round, glittering ball above his hands. The light hung there, suspended by no visible thread; all the same, it wasn't particularly impressive.

Thomas snorted. "You call that magic? That? It's pathetic."

Nick glared at him. "Not good enough for you? How about this?"

He took his hands away from each other, leaving a ball of light dancing in each palm. "Nimafyg!" he roared, and the tiny orbs grew into flickering spheres of wild flame, screaming with power and energy. Nick threw his hands forward, and two separate streams of fire whirled towards Thomas, parting only a centimetre from his nose to avoid his head.

"OK!" Thomas yelped. "You've impressed me!"

Nick grinned, and the flames faded away.

"So," Thomas began hesitantly, fingering the singed remains of his eyebrows. "I've got a ton of magic in me, and since I'm in Mythicia, I can use it, right?"

"Right." agreed Nick.

"Then how the Hell do you know all of this?" Thomas asked.

Nick opened his mouth to reply, but froze as a tumultuous bang snatched the words from his lips.

"I'll explain later. Alex!" he called. "Go see what happened!"

Thomas and Nick waited in tension-locked silence while Alex investigated the source of the explosion. Alex had always been a fast runner, coming first without fail in every speed-based event on Sports Day. And so it was only about a minute before he returned, speaking quickly and loudly.

"Demons!" Alex began, "They must have broken in through the loading bay!"

"How strong?" asked Nick.

"I'd say about level 2 or 3, but there are loads of them. Mostly muticles, but there's something big herding them!"

"Thomas!" Nick called, utterly in control. "Follow me! Let's find out what you can do - we've got some demons to kill!"

Thomas and Nick followed Alex through the gunmetal door and out into a corridor. Thomas stuck very close to Nick - all the new information hurt his head. An hour ago he was headed to double English, and now he was fighting demons!

Nick interrupted Thomas' thoughts. "Be ready," he said in a gruff half-whisper. "This won't look pretty. Since this is your first time in the field, I'll explain. When you see the demons, focus. Don't close your eyes, because something will probably kill you. Imagine the demons dead and, hey presto, they're dead. Always assuming you *do* have magic, and I haven't miscalculated, in which case, you're dead. But you probably have magic... we hope."

Before Thomas could object, Alex shouted back at Thomas.

"Duck!"

Instinctively, Thomas dropped to the ground, just as a ball of billowing flame flashed over his head.

Looking up, he could only blink as a bizarre parody of a jellyfish drifted through the air. It had an eye in the centre of its pulsing body, and the tips of its tentacles burned with crimson fire. One by one, more joined it, its numbers growing with every heartbeat.

"CHARGE!" Alex shouted.

"Is that really necessary?" Nick sighed to himself.

Alex rose swiftly and ran at the advancing swarm, disappearing amongst the gathering demons. Nick fished a small wand from his pocket, which quickly extended into a long staff. A beam of light shot from its tip, incinerating a row of the devilish jellyfish. More swiftly took their place.

"Damn muticles", he muttered as he fired another blast.

Thomas watched out of the corner of his eye as Alex and Nick worked as a team, Nick blasting muticles with his staff, and Alex surfacing from the cloud of monsters only to dive back into the fray, his long knife whirring in impossibly fast spirals, slicing any that got close into bloody discs.

Even so, he hardly saw them. His focus was fixed on the muticles themselves. The sheer impossibility of their existence captivated him. How on earth could such a creature float in the air? Thomas could see no visible wings - the whole structure of its body reminded Thomas of a helium balloon. *Perhaps it's filled with some form of gas?* Thomas thought.

Nick called something between blasts, which Thomas couldn't catch. "Sorry?" he called.

"Hello!" came the reply. "Mythicia to Thomas! How about actually helping fight these wretched things! Magic using time!"

Thomas nervously took a couple of steps towards the nearest muticle as it blasted unsuccessfully at the grinning mage. It swivelled in the air, glaring at Thomas with its single bloodshot eye. The iris expanded, and then a red ray of light shot from the pupil, missing Thomas' head by inches as he ducked to the right. Remembering what Nick had told him, he tried to focus on the demon as he dodged. His hands flared with sudden heat, his fingertips stinging as though pierced with invisible needles, and an odd word popped into his head.

"Hitomas," murmured Thomas. The tingly feeling became a burning sensation. His fingers were almost unbearably hot; at the edges of his vision, he saw that they had turned a bright, fiery red. He raised his palms. A jet of flame erupted from the glowing digits, and before Thomas realised what was happening, the creature was sprawled on the floor, bathed in acrid smoke.

"Way cool." Thomas whispered.

He grinned and lifted his hands towards another of the muticles.

Again, that strange word offered itself up to Thomas' lips. He allowed it to make itself heard, and another blast of fire poured from his fingertips, incinerating another of the jellyfish- like creatures. And yet for every one he killed, two more took its place. But he couldn't give up, not when he was having so much fun.

He turned to see one of the demons floating no more than a few feet behind Nick's head. Its eye flared malevolently, and Thomas just had enough time to shout a garbled warning before the beam of fire burst from its pupil, soaring towards the mage with deadly aim. Nick turned, and raised his hand, catching the beam in his palm with a word of command. He hurled the light back at the muticle, and it exploded with a dull pop and a spurt of bloody goo.

At that moment, a curious changed rippled through the approaching demons. The muticles at the far end of the room were parting, making way for something much, much bigger to come through.

At first, Thomas thought it was a fifteen foot tall, blueish-green lizard, its head covered in similarly coloured writhing snakes, but then he realised that the snakes weren't snakes at all. They were long, snake-like heads attached at the lizard's neck. He drew back from the creature in horror, but still it advanced, the snakes' red eyes searing with terrifying intent.

"My gods...it's a hydra" muttered Nick, suddenly beside him. "They actually managed to capture one. Look, if you can use that flaming hand thing when I say, we can kill it. Alex!" With an astounding burst of speed, Alex struck out with his knife, severing one of the creature's heads before it could react. After a moment, the creature howled, a long, tortured scream, and it reared up on its hind legs, its remaining heads darting forward.

"Quick," cried Nick, "Burn it!"

"Hitomas!" shouted Thomas. Flames leapt from his hands, but he wasn't quick enough. At the stump of the hydra's severed neck, two more heads were slowly growing. The flames blasted the new heads full on, but as the light died Thomas could see the heads remained despairingly uninjured. Its mighty tail whipped round from behind, slamming into Alex's stomach and driving the wind from his lungs. He doubled over, wheezing as it sent him skidding across the floor.

"Damn it," cried Nick, running to his fallen comrade. "Thomas, keep it occupied!" he called. Thomas obliged, sending flame after flame at the hydra as it slashed and darted at him hungrily. Thomas staggered back, ducking under the storm of blows. He turned to see Nick lifting Alex to his feet, taking his eyes momentarily off the creature. It seized the opportunity, its long neck striking forth like a coiled spring, burying its teeth in Thomas' shoulder. He screamed, pain shocking his body and hot blood trickling from the wound as the hydra clamped its jaws down. "Nick!" he shouted through the agony. "Help!"

Nick turned from supporting Alex, his eyes widening as he saw Thomas struggling under the monster's bite. "Nahisth ebesbat!" the mage cried, pointing his staff like a snooker cue. A blast of wind so strong it was almost solid streamed from the baton, hitting the hydra's flank and sending it soaring across the room. Its teeth released Thomas' shoulder, and he gasped with relief as he sank to the floor.

Alex hurried over to Thomas as he lay bleeding on the ground. He placed his hands on the wound. "Nulyfyl," he whispered, and the pain vanished instantly. "Haeldeth owun," the blonde boy said again, and Thomas gasped as the torn flesh knitted together, resealing the gap and staunching the bleeding.

Whilst this was happening, Nick was striking the hydra over and over again with his staff, clubbing the monster's heads with surprising strength. "Come on," he called back. "Try it again!" He leapt backwards as the creature stormed towards Alex, who had drawn his knife. The boy hacked a head off, and this time, Thomas hit the stump with a column of fire. The wound sealed up, cauterised by the heat, making it impossible for another head to grow. Roaring, the creature aimed one of its remaining heads at Thomas, and with a choking, gagging noise it spat a dollop of green bile towards him. He darted to one side, as the floor began to bubble and hiss where the glob had struck.

It reared back to fire again, but jerked as another of its heads was severed by Alex's whirling knife. Thomas sealed the stump with another blast, and the hydra attacked again. This time the creature fired a volley of bile from each of its heads, fanning out across the room in a wide burst. There was no way they could miss.

"Tetropicon!" shouted Nick, as Thomas raised a hand to cover his face in a vague hope to shield himself from the worst of the blast. Instantly, a vast blue bubble formed around the three fighters, sending the globs of acid ricocheting away.

"Ektris!" Alex cried, whilst the creature was busy dodging its own wave of hissing green globs. His knife leapt from his hands and span through the air, severing the hydra's remaining heads. Thomas frantically cast his fire spells, and the stumps sealed up.

Finally, the hydra collapsed backwards, crushing the last of the muticles. A tired silence fell, leaving a gentle ringing in Thomas' ears. All three of them stared at the unmoving corpse of the hydra.

"Did we kill it?" Thomas whispered. He studied the corpse from a distance a few moments longer, noticing it was starting to take on an unhealthy greenish tinge. He turned to ask what it was, and saw Nick and Alex crouching with their hands over their face and ears. "What are you doing?" he asked, but they gave no answer.

The hydra exploded. With a sound like a balloon popping, the thing's skin quite literally ripped itself to pieces, bursting apart in a shower of blood and gore. Thomas could only stand and blink as the foul smelling juices trickled down between his eyes, dripping off the end of his nose.

"Well, that's that then," panted the mage, straightening himself up and wiping a bead of sweat from his aged and wrinkled brow. “Anyone for a cup of tea?”

Chapter 3

Hitomas!

Thomas' head smacked into the ground with an ear-splitting *thunk* as he fell out of his bunk. His head was ringing, and he had had little sleep. He had tossed and turned for over four hours, before finally giving in to his weariness, but even then, he had woken up frequently during the night, until something that might have been a rooster but probably wasn't signified morning.

After the previous night's battle, Thomas had been led back to the room he'd arrived in. The bunk was three beds high, Nick on the bottom, Alex in the middle, and Thomas on the top. As Thomas fell, he couldn't help noticing that Nick wasn't in his bed. He hadn't seen the old mage come in during the night, and wouldn't be surprised if he hadn't slept at all.

"The idea is that you use the ladder," Alex explained, sarcastically, sitting up in bed, fully dressed. He smirked.

Thomas moaned and rolled over. "Shove off," he grunted.

"No need to get cross, just offering friendly advice. Now, come on, up and dressed. Nick's in the library."

"Get dressed into what?" asked Thomas, pulling himself to his feet. "It's not like I got a chance to pack, is it?"

"Your gear's on Nick's bunk. Put it on!"

Thomas glanced over at the bunk, where a large black drawstring bag sat somewhat smugly upon the scattered sheets. He approached it, and somehow it seemed to hold his gaze, daring him to see what hid inside. Suddenly he realised he was having a standoff with a drawstring bag, and hurried up and opened the damn thing.

Inside the bag was a black one-piece jumpsuit, equipped with a chunky kind of phone, in a holster attached to a black belt. Underneath the jumpsuit was a large, bulky backpack and a helmet. Thomas could see no visible zip or opening on the backpack, but it was packed full of something hard and heavy. Curious, he wondered what was inside.

Glancing at Alex, he changed out of his school uniform and slipped the jumpsuit on instead, surprised at its lightness and flexibility. It was like a second skin. He pulled the phone out of its holster, and noticing how much like a gun it looked, pointed it jokingly at Alex. The blonde boy's eyes widened in alarm. "Don't do that!" he shouted warningly. "That's a military issue plasma gun. It'll kill me instantly."

Thomas stared at what he'd assumed to be some sort of phone. They'd given him a weapon. Well, he had known they would be fighting, but somehow being given a gun made the whole thing a lot more... scary.

"Come on!" Alex called before Thomas had time to ponder it further. Alex opened the door and hurried outside, and Thomas had no choice but to swing the backpack onto his shoulders and follow.

They strolled down the corridor, side by side. Like the room, its walls were a shining gunmetal silver. Doors lined the side, but neither sign nor marking indicated what lay beyond them. Alex pushed open the one closest to him, and Thomas found himself inside the biggest library he'd ever seen.

In this room, the walls were made of a soft knotted wood, and rows and rows of bookshelves criss-crossed the library like supermarket aisles. Unsurprisingly, the shelves were full of thousands of books, all different shapes and sizes, and each neatly grouped under their appropriate topics.

Thomas peered down an aisle, and saw it stretched way, way off into the distance, further than his eye could see. It was like stargazing, only with books – the more he looked, the more he saw. Thomas scanned the nearest, seeing *"100 Basic Invisibility Spells"* and *"A Grand Almanac of the creatures of Lascar 3"* amongst the thousands of titles.

Nick was seated by a table down one of the aisles, flicking through a large leathery tome entitled *"Prophecies of the 15th Age"*. "Destined, Destined, Destined..." he was murmuring to himself as he scanned the pages.

Alex cleared his throat. Nick span around, tensed. Seeing Alex and Thomas, he relaxed. "Ah, Alex, Thomas. It's good to see you."

"Er... morning," Thomas said.

"I'm sure you have lots of questions," Nick said. "And I'm ready to do my best to answer them."

Thomas glanced at Alex. There was so much he wanted to know – so much he didn't understand. But he had to start somewhere. "How do you know so much about Mythicia?" he asked. "You can't have been here for more than a year, but you seem like you've lived here for ages."

It was Nick's turn to glance at Alex, who nodded, the two sharing a hidden message.

Nick studied Thomas carefully, and began, "Alex and I, Thomas..."

"Yes?" Thomas replied.

"We're very old. Alex is technically only twenty five years younger than me. But he... changed. Accident with a time-space manipulator, long story."

Thomas looked at Nick quizzically. The information was coming so fast, it was baffling to say the least. "You mean, when you were at school with me, you were adults?"

Nick cocked his head. "Well, yes, technically. We used glamour – magic that changed our appearances. It fitted our cover story to appear as young boys. But we still wouldn't have been as old as we are now. You see, time passes differently in Mythicia. Faster than it does on Earth. I would imagine for you, I was missing for, say, a year?"

Thomas nodded.

"Time runs at a faster rate in Mythicia. For us, it was six years."

"What?" asked Thomas.

"Six years. Not a particularly nice six years, either. Lots of fights, lots of death, that sort of thing. They aged me. But they didn't age Alex. He'll stay young forever, whilst I appear as a man of my true age – sixty three."

"Weird," breathed Thomas, amazed. "But why were you on Earth in the first place?"

Nick smiled. "We were searching for something."

"And did you find it?"

Nick snapped his book shut. He whispered something, and it floated up and positioned itself back in its rightful place on its shelf. "That's enough questions for now," he said. "Thomas, come with me!"

Nick strode out the wooden door they had come in through. Alex called after him.

"I'll catch up with you guys later. I just need to read up on something."

Nick nodded, and marched up to the metal door on the opposite side of the corridor. Thomas followed him.

Nick put his hand on the door.

"Ilcasimo," he hissed. It swung open, leading to a flight of steps spiralling downwards.

Nick led Thomas down the steps, his sandalled feet clicking across the carved stone. They were treacherous indeed – some were hard and rough, but others were smooth and had been worn away. Thomas had to be careful not to lose his footing, but Nick descended them with a certain serene grace.

As they hurried deeper into the ground, Thomas had another thought. "Nick, what are you?" he asked.

"I beg your pardon?" the mage replied.

"Well, you said all humans are on Earth, but you and Alex were born here. So what are you?"

Nick stopped, and Thomas almost carried on straight into his back. The mage turned and looked at Thomas. "My father was an elf," he said. "And my mother was a wood nymph. I'm not sure what that makes me. Alex's mother was an elf, though."

"What was his father?"

Nick didn't reply.

"Where are we going, anyway?" Thomas asked.

"Training," replied Nick

"What training?" replied Thomas.

Nick ignored him. *We'll just have to wait and see,* Thomas thought.

They turned left through a large metal door at the bottom of the stairs. "For this training, we must be a lot deeper underground than the rest of the base is," he said.

"Why?"

"Because it's a training room, and in the training room we stretch our magical powers to the limit. Doing that results in a fairly sizeable" and here the mage jerked both his clasped hands away from each other, "*kaboom*".

Thomas shut up. They came to the end of the stairs, which continued straight into a thick metal door. Nick made another hissing sound, and the door swung open. Thomas stepped into a very large room. At one end was a row of blackened cardboard cut-outs in the shapes of various different creatures with wings, tentacles and all sorts of horrible mutations. At the other end was an altar - a large stone rock, the head of a snake leering from its peak, and hundreds of strange patterns carved into its base.

"Put your hand on the altar," commanded Nick

Thomas did as he was asked, and was surprised to feel a strange warmth pulsing through it, as if the stone itself was alive. After a moment, the markings on the altar began to pulse in different colours. One glowed red, one blue, one white, one brown, one yellow; pretty much every colour of the rainbow had a symbol. One even seemed to drain the light from the air around it, to such a degree that it somehow *glowed black.*

As the colours flickered and pulsed, the shadows in the corners of the room seemed to grow, rising up the walls like leering giants. With a sparking, hissing sound, the already dim lights swinging from the ceiling flickered, and the air was suddenly very cold. Thomas shivered as his breath misted in front of him, and a peculiar smell of burning billowed into his nose. Without warning, a bolt of shooting pain soared up his arm and he snapped his hand away from the altar like it had bitten him. And then, as if a switch had been flicked, the shadows retreated, the air warmed, the altar stopped glowing, and the room returned to normal again.

"What happened?" asked Thomas, suddenly filled with an

inexplicable feeling of dread.

"You were recognised," Nick said, tapping the altar with his staff. "This is an Asgardian Magi Extrapolator. It draws upon the power of a mage and reveals through the colours of the symbols what magical Disciplines they are capable of mastering."

"Disciplines?" Thomas asked, intrigued, but also wary of the emphasised "D" .

"Types of magic. Look, let me show you." Nick leant forward and placed his own crinkled hand on the altar. As he did so, four of the symbols lit up across the stone, one red, one blue, one white and one brown. This time, however, the room remained exactly how it always had been, and no feeling of dread loomed over Thomas' thoughts.

As Nick removed his hand, he smiled. "Did you notice how those four symbols lit up? Each one represents a Discipline. My four were the four basic elements – Water, Earth, Fire and Air. It's very rare for a mage to have more than three Disciplines; my master was very pleased when he discovered I could learn four."

But Thomas' mind was already reliving what had happened when *he* had put his hand on the altar. Every symbol had glowed. Every single one.

"Nick," he said. "Does that mean I can master *every* Discipline?"

Nick's smile widened, and he nodded. "Yes, you can."

"So, I can use any spell I want?" But Nick shook his head. "That's not how it works. You can't just use every Discipline you're capable of from the word go. You were born with Fire, so of course you can use that. But the others, you'll find you can't control. Try Water – the word is "Laqsa" Nick ignored the liquid that suddenly pooled by his feet.

Thomas nodded, and repeated the word. His mind whirled, and a wave of nausea flooded through him. He coughed, and a spray of water shot from his mouth, splashing to the floor with a splatter.

"And now we'll have to dry you off, I suppose," Nick sighed.

"Dry me off?" Thomas started to ask, but looked down to see his jumpsuit sodden from head to toe. A large droplet formed on the tip of his nose, and after a long moment, fell to the ground with a *"plink!"*

"And that'll continue to happen every time you try to use a Discipline you haven't mastered until the prophecy sorts itself out. But that's not important right now. Hitomas Cęoduntri!" A warm and soothing heat worked its way up from Thomas' toes, and within seconds he was dry. He grinned. Nick stepped over the still forming puddle and walked across the floor.

Thomas called him back – he remembered the symbol that had glowed black; obviously it represented a Discipline, but what magic could make darkness glow?

"Nick, what Discipline did the black one show?"

Nick turned, and suddenly his face was grave. "That's dark, dark stuff, Thomas. The black symbol is Death magic. It's only taught at the ARCON academy on Hades IV, and I hope that's one place you'll never have to visit."

At that, Nick turned and strode over to one of the cut-outs. "This is your target. You must stand here-" he raised his staff, and a glowing blue line of fire ran across the floor at the other end of the room. "- and cast your flame spell at the cut-out. It's a simple exercise. Get it right, and we'll move onto something else."

Thomas took a few nervous steps towards the flickering line. He focused, as he had done in the fight against the muticles. His hands began to feel hot and tingly. Looking at them, he saw that they were bright red. He pointed them at the first cut-out. A few sparks burst out of his hands, but guttered out. Nothing else.

"What?" cried Thomas. He tried again. More sparks.

"It's because," explained Nick, "Your magic only kicked in when your life was threatened. It was your body's natural reaction. When you feel threatened, your brain says go! But when you're talking to me here, you brain says stop! The problem will go away when you've had some decent experience with magic, but until then, you're stuck. So, I've brought along a little help with that. Here we go!"

The earth shook, and an almighty crack echoed throughout the room. Then, as if it had always been there, a sort of man - thing was standing by Nick's side.

"This is Specimen 1. He is the only known demon that works for the Alliance. He's a level 1 doom hunter."

The "Doom hunter" looked mostly like something Thomas had seen on TV. Simply a tall, spindly man, clad from head to foot in black cloth.

"He *is* a demon, only he's also the most humanoid kind of demon there is. But just to warn you, *don't* take off his mask. They're incredibly sensitive to light!

"What do you mean "level 1"?" asked Thomas

"The alliance ranks demons from levels one to five, one being the weakest, five being the strongest. I've given you a weak one both to start you off, and because it's the only one we have. Now, enough questions. Begin!"

Thomas opened his mouth to ask what on earth Nick meant, but immediately closed it again as the doom hunter struck. It moved lightning fast, flipping towards him, claws (not even girls had nails as long as that) outstretched.

Thomas' hands instantly shot up in defence, sparks leaping from his outstretched digits, and the demon fell backwards, hissing like an angry cat. Thomas saw no expression behind its black cloth mask, but he had the feeling it was both surprised and enraged. It flexed its knees and darted forward again, closing its hands around Thomas' neck before he knew what was happening. He shouted out as the hands tightened their grip, squeezing his windpipe and cutting off his breath.

"Stop!" commanded Nick, and the demon halted, releasing Thomas and casting him to the floor and strutting back to the mage's side. "Can you think of anything you did against the muticles that you're not doing here? You barely scorched S - 1, and he's only level 1. Think!"

Thomas thought. He thought back to the fight with the muticles. He remembered focusing as Nick had told him, clearing his mind of his worries. He told Nick so.

"Good!" the mage enthused, grinning. "But what else?"

Thomas had said something, hadn't he? It had just, sort of, popped into his head. What was it, now? Ah yes, it had sounded like his name - *Tomas*. Something - *tomas...*

"Hitomas!" Thomas exclaimed.

A stream of fire burst forth from his hand, whipping through the air and fanning out like a tornado. Thomas grinned and began to turn, carrying the stream of fire around with him as he pivoted. He pointed it at one of the targets, and willed it to grow to engulf it. As if it was one with his mind, the flames seared forth, blazing through the cut-out and leaving only ashes in its wake. Thomas laughed out loud, but the laugh turned to a frown as the fire widened again, shooting strands of energy out across the room.

The column of heat billowed, and spat a mighty whiplash of flame around in a circle, striking Nick across the arm. Thomas tried to cut the fire off, but realised he had no idea how. The flames were growing bigger now, threatening to burst loose. He started to panic, trying to point the flame to safe place, but Nick cursed, and lifted his staff. "Laqsa!" he countered, and a wave of water erupted from his staff, and extinguished Thomas' fire.

"As much as I am glad that you have learnt the True Speak word for "fire," Nick said, clutching his scorched arm, "I would prefer it if you didn't burn down my training room!"

"Sorry, Nick," Thomas said, but he didn't really mean it. The sheer thrill he got from using magic was terrific. But then he remembered the panic and knew he had lost control of the flames, and wondered how much damage he could potentially have done had Nick not stepped in at the final moment. He hadn't meant to hurt him, but the flames had moved of their own accord, singeing through the cloth and burning Nick's skin. The mage whispered a few words as he clutched at his arm, and the blotchy marks faded away, leaving the skin as good as new. Thomas was suddenly reminded of something Nick had mentioned. "What was that you said?" Thomas asked Nick. "True Speak. What's that?"

"True Speak is the language of magic," Nick said. "It was spoken by the elves millennia ago, but then one of the spiky eared fools did something silly, and the result was that every word became imbued with power. Hitomas was the True Speak word for 'fire.'" At this point the mage's robes began to smoke, and he yelped as he pulled his hand from within one of its pockets. As he held it up to his face, Thomas saw it was wreathed in glittering flames. "But as you can see, no one can say it without making something combust. The same principal applies to the rest of the words in True Speak. Obviously the elves abandoned the language as soon as the magic started, but we magi still use it. Every word causes something to change depending on the phrasing, and of course the meaning. So you can trigger that fire spell using a combination of emotional stimulus and the True Speak word. Now you can have a proper fight with S-1."

Thomas nodded, and murmured the spell.

The demon leapt.

As the flames leapt from Thomas' hand, the demon jerked to one side, the fire missing by centimetres. Its deadly claws flew towards Thomas' face, but Thomas ducked, and rolled out the way, the blades slicing through the air where Thomas had been a moment before. But S-1 didn't slow, flipping over Thomas' head and slashing its claws downwards, grazing Thomas' cheek. He winced as the hot blood trickled down his face.

A sudden rage engulfed Thomas' mind and leaping to his feet, he hurled a fireball straight at the demon's now exposed back. Even as the flames left Thomas' fingertips, it spun around to face him, bending its legs to leap again. But not quick enough. The flames caught it full in the face, and the sheer momentum of the fire hurled it across the room.

It hit the wall, slid down to the ground, and lay still. Thomas cautiously approached it. It didn't move, looking almost happy in its sleep. Unconscious, it didn't seem nearly so threatening. A sudden curiosity overcame Thomas, and he reached tentatively forward. "Don't-" Nick started, but it was too late. Thomas pulled the mask down.

The demon screamed. A mass of purplish-cream tentacles writhed out from S-1's face, twisting and snapping at the air as the ear-piercing screech blasted at Thomas' face. No eyes or mouth were visible amongst the spiked tendrils, but even without any features, the creature's pain was obvious. Thomas winced, and gently lifted the mask back up over the writhing mass. The creature fell silent, as peaceful as a sleeping child.

"I'd rather you hadn't done that," Nick said quietly. "He won't wake for at least a week now. Light is perilous to their nervous system – it burns the nerve endings, leading to intense pain."

"I'm sorry," replied Thomas.

"Dispelocran diiman." Nick commanded, and the unconscious demon vanished.

"Other than that," Nick the mage continued, suddenly cheerful, "You did a good job. I must congratulate you on that finishing strike – a perfect shot. Now," Nick paused, whispered something, and the cut-outs vanished. "As well as learning to defeat demons, you must be prepared to fight by our mythical allies. The alliance is more than our humble group, Thomas. It is a network of freedom fighters scattered all over Mythicia. We've received word from the rebel base in Atlantis; I sent them a report the moment you arrived, and they've dispatched a group to meet you here. They should be arriving in a few days. But let's not think about then, let's think about *now.* On with the training!"

Thomas spent the rest of the day blasting targets, reading textbooks, and sparring with Nick. Finally, after hours of gruelling training, he was allowed to retire to his room, where he flopped onto his bunk and fell immediately into a deep, dreamless sleep.

Chapter 4

The Destined

It is a well-known fact that large bodies of mass such as planets and asteroids are formed by gravity. Pieces of disconnected rock and junk float aimlessly in the void of space, before eventually, due to the force of attraction that exists amongst all objects of matter, they begin to clump around the largest. More often than not, this is merely a larger chunk of rock, however in certain circumstances it has been known that something far from rocky has formed such a core. For instance, in minotauran lore, it is believed that Daedalus I, the spiritual homeworld of the minotaur, formed around the great god Gargath, who in his contemplation strayed too far into an asteroid belt, and so soon found himself trapped at the centre of what was to become the planet. The belief then formed that one day he would free himself, but whilst all that was irrelevant religious babble, the fact remains that the planet formed around an entity. And so it is not too difficult to accept that another planet could have formed around a superentity. One such as, for instance, the planet Arcfied.

Mythician cuisine was certainly an interesting experience for Thomas. Having grown up in a world populated with cows, pigs, chickens, and other such edible livestock, naturally his taste buds had become accustomed to their flavours. When he was four years old, an aunt of his had turned vegetarian, and he'd wondered how on earth she'd managed it. To subject oneself to a diet of plants for the rest of one's life seemed an impossible and even pointless feat. And yet somehow, staring at the gently bubbling globules of flesh on his plate, he had a sudden urge to join her.

"Military issue synthetic meat 87a. Jackalope flavour," Alex said, grinning across the table at Thomas' expression. "We thought, since a jackalope's essentially a rabbit with antlers, it might be easier to stomach for you."

Thomas prodded a lump cautiously with his fork. It was of an off-pink hue, like an extremely rare steak, although far weaker, breaking apart at the merest touch. "Synthetic?" he asked.

"Grown. The Empire seized control of practically all the farm allotments in the known universe when it took over. All meat was diverted to supplying the demons' ranks. Anything we want has to be artificially grown from stem cells. And like most fakes, it's only about a tenth as good as the real thing."

"What about vegetables?"

"Nick's got a green-house on site. All rebel high-rankers go through a special gardening module. We haven't got anything quite ready at the moment though, we're harvesting the day after tomorrow. So go on, you gonna try it or what?"

"I guess so," Thomas muttered, scooping a fork full of the pinkish flesh off the plate and into his mouth. Surprisingly, it wasn't that bad. In fact, he'd even go so far as to say it was good. It tasted like nothing he'd ever eaten before, but if he had to make a comparison, he'd have to say it was closest to lobster.

"That's actually pretty nice," he said after swallowing. Alex stared at him.

"Serious?"

"Yeah. Really, I like it." To underline the point, he took another mouthful. And then another.

"What do they feed you on Earth? 'Cos that stuff is rank, truly rank. And you say it's nice. Wait till you try it from an actual jackalope, I reckon you might just die."

Thomas grinned. "So what's for pudding?"

With a noise like a giant sneezing, the table collapsed. The ground shook and rocked, as a shockwave crashed through the base, sending Thomas and Alex sprawling to the floor. A great cloud of dust burst out of the ceiling, even as Alex flipped to his feet, steadying himself on one of the kitchen walls. Thomas' head throbbed with the cacophony of noise, scattering his mind as he scrabbled on the floor. Somehow Alex managed to stagger over to Thomas through the turmoil, haul him up, and drag him towards the door. "Where are we going?" shouted Thomas over the clamour.

"To see Nick!" Alex replied "There are never earthquakes on Arcfied – it's too small a planet!"

They stumbled down the corridor, and entered the library. True enough, Nick was there, desperately scanning a tome for some kind of explanation with his left hand, and shielding himself from falling debris with his right. He cursed violently as *"An Earthquake Survival Guide,"* bounced off his head.

"If this book is correct" he explained, "This is no earthquake. The planet Arcfied is only really a big asteroid, and it hasn't got a core of any description. Therefore, there are no convection currents, which of course means an earthquake is a complete impossibility. I suggest we get out of here now, before it gets-"

He was cut off mid-sentence as a distinct crack echoed through the room. A hole was beginning to open in the centre of one of the aisles. Alex was right next to it at the time, and screamed as the edge of the ground beneath his right foot crumbled away into widening gap. Thomas coughed as dust erupted into the air, whipping around the room like a tornado.

The quaking grew more violent, and several of the bookshelves began to wobble threateningly, sending their cargo of knowledge tumbling from their embrace.

"Take cover!" shouted Nick, as one of the shelves crashed to the ground, books catapulting into the air.

The ceiling groaned ominously, causing Thomas' eyes to dart upwards. A brief curse left his lips and he started to shout a warning, but even as he did so the roof splintered to pieces under the strain of the shaking. Thomas yelped as part of the collapsing ceiling narrowly missed his head in its uninterrupted plummet to the floor. With a sound that can only be described as "thwick!" the shard of ceiling buried itself in the ground, sticking up like a great monstrous tooth.

"Ergai akmist tęg fallq!" Nick yelled, raising one arm and covering his eyes with the other. A coil of blue lightning crackled through the air, freezing the falling fragments motionless, hanging like... like nothing Thomas had ever seen. With a flick of his wrist, Nick lowered them gently to the floor, where they could do no damage.

Then, as abruptly as it had begun, the quaking stopped. Thomas hung dizzily onto the edge of an aisle, his head spinning and his heart beating with the rhythm of a thousand drums. As his mind cleared, he heard Nick gasp with relief, and watched him survey the wreckage that was once a library.

Lodged inside the gaping crack was a great tablet made of goldish-bronze rock. A thin shaft of light from a hole in the ceiling glinted off something red and shiny, sticking out of the top of the stone. On the first look, Thomas saw it as the glint of a blood-red eye, glaring malevolently from the top of the tablet, but when he looked again it glittered like a star. And on his third look Thomas saw it for what it really was - a ruby.

The ruby was embedded in the hilt of a sword. The hilt was made of a strange shining metal, and looked very heavy. The actual blade was still inside the rock, with only the grip visible, but even showing such little of the weapon, its beauty was clear. Alex took a cautious step towards the hilt, but Nick raised a hand and stopped him.

"I should go." he insisted. "It could be dangerous."

As he walked up to the stone, he noticed a thin line of golden writing inscribed upon the hilt in True Speak.

"It says "Hestine Deford", meaning 'For the Destined,'" the mage translated. His eyes flashed, and a grin lit up his face, beaming with satisfaction. He grabbed the jewel encrusted hilt with both hands, and pulled.

Nothing happened.

Both perplexed and excited, he pulled again.

Still nothing.

"Just as I thought!" he declared, the ruby's reflection dancing in his eyes.

"I think Thomas should have a go," suggested Alex, winking at Nick. Not for the first time, Thomas was taken by the belief that the mage and his apprentice were keeping something from him.

"Indeed," Nick said, returning the wink. "Thomas!"

Thomas uncertainly stepped towards the stone. A sort of calming aura radiated from its hilt, and for a strange moment Thomas almost felt as if it were calling to him. Nick and Alex waited with baited breath as he reached out and took the beautiful hilt with both hands.

The handle felt rough and textured against his palms; not so much that it would be uncomfortable, but just enough so he could grip it with ease. He tightened his hold on the hilt, and suddenly he knew that whatever was happening now was *right*. The sword was meant for him, and for him it would be released from its stone prison. He paused, took a deep breath, and pulled.

The rock split with a tremendous *crack*.

The sword came free.

"I knew it..." Nick muttered under his breath. "This is what we've been waiting for, Alex. We've found our Destined..."

Thomas shifted the sword from one hand to the other. The sword was amazingly light to hold, and the blade itself was just as beautiful as the hilt. The metal was the silver of the moon, honed to such an incredible sharpness that as he stabbed upwards, the air seemed to part around the weapon, sliced in two by its piercing point.

Grinning, he flourished it, twirling the blade in a broad circle, before spinning around and thrusting it through an imaginary foe. He stabbed it into the ground, and almost fell over as it sank straight through the solid floor as though it was water.

Alex, meanwhile, had picked up a thin piece of the broken rock that formed a gravelly carpet across the library floor. The exquisite rug that had covered the floor before was wrecked, ripped to tatters by the half-collapse of the building. Alex had been there when Nick had had it built, and knew both how much the place meant to the old mage, and how much emotion Nick was trying to hide. Nick carried an impeccable pride with him wherever he went, and signs of weakness such as tears rarely showed. Something caught Alex's eye as he weighed the stone in his palm, and he looked down sharply. A few words were gouged into the rock, and he raised his eyebrows in surprise to see they were written in New Elfish. He read them quietly to himself.

"When the Destined claims his sword from its rest,

His life doth depend on passing the test.

The beast must be slain using this blade,

For that is its purpose, for which it was made."

He called Nick over, handing him the stone. The elderly mage squinted at it suspiciously, muttering the words to himself as he scanned the text. "What's it talking about?" Nick asked, not to Alex, it seemed, but to the world around him. "What beast?" he speculated. "What test?"

As if to answer his question, the rumbling started again. Thomas, still fiddling with the sword, sweeping it through the air and lunging with it like a fencer, dropped the blade with a clatter. Hastily, he snatched it up, and steadied himself against a bookshelf. Alex and Nick did the same, clinging both to each other and to the wooden aisles. The great crack in the floor, now exposed again as the rock plugging it had been shattered, slowly began to widen.

Nick extended his staff and pointed it at the hole threateningly, and as if in challenge an inhuman screech emitted from within the black chasm, which was now wide enough to hold a large trampoline, if one were in such a way inclined to test it. Nick's hand remained steady, the staff unmoving as a ghoulish hand reached out of the pit and groped the edge.

"I think we're about to find out!" Alex called, flexing his fingers.

What little skin that was left on the hand was red, but much of it was flayed, so Thomas could see pale brown bone showing clearly through the torn skin. The hand grabbed a hold on a fallen bookshelf, and gripped it tight. As the bare tendons pulled taught, inch by inch, a dark, tall, monstrous creature hauled itself out of the pit. In shape, it resembled a colossal winged skeleton. Mammoth tusks stuck out of its filthy jaw, and jagged, bony wings extended from its broad shoulders. Decaying flesh was draped across the thing's body, and miniature burning torches flickered and crackled in its otherwise empty eye sockets. A long, creaking roar erupted from its acid dripping mandibles, bolts of crackling electricity darting up the creature's spine and along its ribs. As the monster leaned forward hungrily, the stench of rotting meat on its breath was overpowering.

Nick was the first to retaliate. "Hitomas!" he cried, raising his staff high into the air. A great pulsing ball of fire soared from the staff's tip, shooting towards the thing's chest, but it batted the flames away like a tennis ball. The red sphere blazed down into the ground, setting fire to what was left of the library carpet. Nick winced. "Not the Persian rug," he moaned. The creature ignored him and took a mighty step forward, lifting a hideous claw.

"For Odmehlwor!" Alex roared, the flames' reflection glittering in the pools of his eyes. He unsheathed his knife and charged at the monster, not the slightest bit intimidated by its horrifying form. The apprentice reached the monster and leapt into the air, stabbing furiously at the creature's bones as he searched for a weak point. The thing's mighty skull swivelled, and stared at Alex with its flaming red eyes, piercing him with a gaze of utter malice. Slowly and calmly, it extended a claw and wrapped it around his waist. He gasped with surprise and fear as the monster lifted him up into the air and close to its skull. It plucked the knife from Alex's hand with a pair of iron hard fingers and tossed the weapon away.

"The sword!" cried Nick, "Thomas, use it! I think it's the only thing that can hurt it!"

The creature struck down with its free claw, missing Thomas' leg by inches. "What is that thing?" called Thomas, "Some kind of demon?"

"Yep." Nick replied as Thomas rolled to avoid another hit. "It's an archfiend. A primordial entity, one of the first demons that ever existed – be careful, it looks livid. Someone hasn't had his coffee this morning," he added under his breath.

Thomas leapt to his feet, and sidestepped to avoid a blast of fire which spewed from the creature's mouth. He cried out as the flames licked his trouser leg, scorching the black material. And then, in a feat of bravery that surprised even himself, he pointed his blade at the monster, and ran forward. The archfiend opened its terrifying mouth once again, another stream of flame gushing forth at Thomas' frightened form. He hurled himself to the floor, and the fire shot over his head, so close that he could feel their heat on his back.

He leapt to his feet, and ran the last few steps towards the creature. The archfiend smacked a claw down and Thomas slid beneath its arch, but one of the wicked nails nicked the skin of his thigh, drawing a long line of blood across his lower leg. He kept sliding across the damaged floor, and found himself staring up at the beast's colossal form. His head was at the height of the creature's lower torso, so that was where he struck. With a cry of "Hitomas!" setting his blade alight, he drove it upwards into the archfiend's chest. Blue fire flickered around the razor sharp edges, and the creature screamed as its ribs were split open. For a long moment, the creature swayed, looking as if it was about to topple, but then the fires flared in its eyes and it surged forward. One of its great claws swept Nick aside, whilst the other reached out, and picked Thomas up. He struggled, but the skeletal hand held him firm. The grip tightened. Thomas screamed.

A gunshot echoed through the ruined library.

The thing's grip loosened, and Thomas fell to the floor. The archfiend crashed to the ground, and behind it stood a solitary figure, dressed in bright blue armour like that of a space marine, smoke curling from the barrel of the automatic machine gun cradled in the person's gauntleted hands.

The figure stood tall and proud in front of a door sized hole in the wall behind him. It had been deliberately cut using some strange kind of laser-tool.

The blue helmet slid back, revealing a young, healthy face. The person, it seemed, was the same age as Alex, and was the same height too. He had long, wispy, silver hair, and his eyes were a startlingly bright blue. Thomas knew that, had the young man existed on earth, he would have been a model, or a film star, or anything that required good looks - the boy was flawless in every way.

"An elf..." murmured Nick.

"All right?" greeted the elf.

He was soon joined by six more of his kind, marching in through the same smoking hole in the wall that the first had obviously come through. Only the first had his helmet off. The young elf walked up to the cowering group of magi, and spoke.

"Lieutenant Silvanus, leader of Rebel squad 214 reporting for duty *general*!"

Nick blinked. "General?" he asked. "I'm sorry, but there must have been a mistake. I'm not a general."

"You are now. The demons recently took the rebel base on Garactoid. They left no survivors. Unfortunately, that means we lost General Boar. You were the rank below him, thus you now have his status, sir."

Nick nodded. "Very well, soldier! Now, state the purpose of you visit. I very much doubt you came to save us from that little archfiend problem we had back there," he laughed nervously, a bead of sweat forming on his brow.

"No, you are correct, that is not the purpose of our "visit", as you put it. Our true purpose is to escort your squadron to the central base on Entropia. Malcaractimus knows where you are. You let a muticle escape in the last assault; the demons will find you, and they will destroy you. They never leave any survivors—you know that. We'd better leave right now. Get your stuff, and meet back here again in ten minutes!"

"Right!" began Nick "Do what he says!"

Thomas and Alex walked quickly to their room. Thomas grabbed his bag off his bed, and quickly changed into his gear. It was tight and fitted snugly around his body, the leggings reaching down past his ankles and held fast by straps to his shoes, and the sleeves ending in sealed gloves. For the first time, he lifted the sleek black helmet out of his pack, and fitted it over his head. The mirrored visor darkened his view at first, but then it cleared, like a pair of transition-lenses. After Alex had done the same, they hurried back to the library.

"Wait," Silvanus said, raising a hand. "General, where's the Destined? You promised me a master to take back to Prometheus; I hope for your sake you're not going to disappoint. Where've you hidden him?"

Nick coughed, and gestured meaningfully at Thomas. Silvanus' eyes widened in both surprise and disbelief. "No..." he murmured. "That halfling is the Destined?"

"Human, Silvanus. He is a human child, and I am lead to believe he is the Destined the prophecy speaks of."

Thomas grabbed Nick's arm. "What are you talking about? What do you mean Destined?" he asked frantically.

"Show the Lieutenant your sword, Thomas."

Thomas stared at him for a moment, and then slowly, he drew his sword from its scabbard and stepped closer to Silvanus, aware of the gaze of all the elves on him. Silvanus inspected the text carved into the hilt. Then he looked up, right in to Thomas' eyes, and sank down to one knee, and the rest of the soldiers followed suit. Grinning, Alex and Nick knelt too.

"My liege," he whispered, although a tinge of bitterness hung on the edge of his words. "I have sinned greatly to doubt you; it is true I am not worthy to touch your sword. My gun is at your command in repentance."

Thomas blinked, his mouth hanging wide open. Potential replies jostled for position in his head, but none survived to reach his lips. To his relief, Nick came to his rescue, standing and moving to his side. "Rise, Lieutenant Silvanus. I'm sure you have the Destined's forgiveness. Come, we must go."

Silvanus shook himself, and jumped to his feet. Instantly, the elves rose with him. "Let's move!" Silvanus commanded. The blue-armoured soldiers marched outside, moving in perfect unison. Silvanus had rehearsed them well. Nick, Alex and Thomas hurried after them, the shocked "Destined" sheathing his sword as he ran.

Alex nudged Thomas. "Hit the red button on your helmet," he explained. "It gives you oxygen inside the visor—you'll need it. The air on Arcfied is toxic to humans. The suit'll protect you, but don't take anything off for any reason. It really won't be very healthy." Thomas nodded, reaching up to his helmet, running his fingers over the smooth metal until they caught on the rubbery circular button. It was simple enough to press. "When I say go," Alex continued, "pull the string on your backpack."

"Why?" asked Thomas.

"Just do it."

They stepped out onto the meteor-pockmarked surface of the planet, leaving the artificial gravity of the base behind them and striding forth into near-weightlessness. It was the most peculiar sensation. Every step felt like a dream, surreal and unnatural.

It barely affected the others – Nick, Alex and the elves simply adjusted their stride and bounced about a foot into the air with every step. Thomas, however, stayed standing in the entrance, goggling at the starry blackness of space and the sheer concept of standing on another world. "Come on!" Nick called back to him. "We haven't got time for you to gape at every crater on the ruddy planet! Get a move on!"

Thomas took a few more tentative steps, still confused by the sudden weightlessness and surprised as he floated through the air with every stride. "Where are we going?" Thomas shouted.

"There's a transport ship just above the cloud layer," Silvanus replied. "If we can get to it in time, we should be all right."

"In time for what?"

But Silvanus didn't have to reply. The answer had already revealed itself in its horrific glory. As the squad ran forward, a great cloud of things that were familiar in a terrifyingly bad way drifted down through the crimson cloud layer. Muticles.

With the coordination of a Roman legion, the fiery fog began to descend upon the group of rebels. "Pull the string." muttered Alex, quietly.

Thomas pulled.

Two metal cylinders slid out from either side of his backpack with a click. Before Thomas could turn his head to look, two huge jets of flame erupted from holes in their curved ends. Thomas yelled with fear as he was launched into the air with the speed of a cannonball.

"Surely we're not going *towards* them? They're *demons*!" he cried as he struggled to turn himself round, but to no avail.

They sped towards the swirling fog, which only continued to advance with terrifying speed. An array of crimson light burst forward from the descending monsters, searing the very air they flew through. Two elves immediately dropped out of the clouds, screaming as they fell.

"Return fire!" ordered Silvanus.

The reaction was instantaneous. Before Thomas could blink, a blitz of plasma bolts erupted from the long barrels of the squad's blasters. The swarm parted, and the group accelerated through the opening. The demons reacted by closing in on the small army, cutting them off.

Thomas turned his head, this way and that, searching desperately for another escape route. In his mind's eye, he could see another wave of concentrated flames thundering out of the creatures' single, bloodshot eyes, burning the entire group to nothing but ashes. Snapping back to reality, he saw Alex withdraw something small and black out of his pocket, and toss it towards the muticles.

"What's that?" called Thomas over the howling wind.

"It's a maelstrom-grenade, now cover your ears!"

A ball of pure lightning forced its way out of the dark, metallic shell, accompanied by a deafening boom and a bone-juddering throb. As the smoke cleared, at least half the muticles began a long spiral towards the awaiting ground, splattering into the pockmarked dirt like rain.

The remaining monsters fanned out, spreading apart in a great sweeping arc to surround the escaping rebels. The elves' barrage of plasma continued, but they did little to dent the indefatigable advance of the demonic ranks. Streak after streak of deadly fire lanced from their malice-filled pupils, and another elf plummeted to his doom, the ray leaving a glistening hole in his forehead.

"This has gone on long enough," Nick called. "Cover me for a moment!"

Responding to the command, the elves adjusted their angle of flight so that they formed a circle around Nick, protecting him as he drew his staff from inside his robes and extended it. "Hitomas gargantuatem mentarom laqsa. Rethrol intaverok lucyamira awhanlem!"

Even as the words left his mouth, Thomas sensed something change in the world around him. The colours seemed to brighten, like someone turning up the contrast on a computer monitor; the sky distorted to a frightening blue. But most of all, Nick himself seemed to grow for a moment, whilst somehow staying the same size, his presence inflating across the battlefield. His staff burst into flickering flame, the earth of the ground below shattered into shards which rose and formed into a circle around his body, water droplets condensed out of the air and froze into knife-sharp blades, and a mighty wind drew up great columns of dust which shimmered around his elderly frame. This was the power of the mage, Thomas realised. This was magic at its most powerful.

"Calbereth Sitor!"

Then there was only light, so bright that even when Thomas closed his eyes it made no difference. Shining white, icy cold, piercing his very mind. It lasted a mere three or four seconds, but when it cleared, leaving his retinas screaming in agony, not a single muticle remained. Not a trace was left of their existence, except perhaps for faint shadows hovering in the air where once they had floated, and even they vanished after a moment's silence.

Nick crumpled in the air, hanging from his jetpack and swaying as it flew. An elf dropped out of formation and grabbed hold of him, steering him onwards towards...

"The ship!" Silvanus shouted.

Sure enough, out of the blazing sky descended something which

Thomas had only seen in films. It was a spaceship. The great titan of metal resembled a giant, flying stag beetle. Huge turbine engines propelled its disk shaped body forward, and its pincers waited to obliterate any demons unlucky enough to be caught in their steel grasp. A large metal plaque triumphantly announced the name of the ship—"*Space Beetle*".

A ramp gently lowered itself from the ship's underside on metal rods, red lights twinkling on either side.

"In there!" came the order.

They flew closer and closer to the ship, the entrance ramp slowly dominating Thomas' vision. Just before Thomas could reach the ramp, however, a great red blast split the group of escapees in two.

They were being pursued.

Another ship, which completely dwarfed the *Beetle*, was rising up behind them. It was a blood-crimson colour, purple wings extending from its armoured sides and black turbines mounted beneath its iron underbelly. Mounted at the very front of the ship was a mighty black cannon, still smoking from the blast that had almost killed the rebels for good. Thomas could just make out its name – *"The Emperor's Wrath"*, written in midnight black on the dark red hull. It fired again, but this time, the group was ready. They swooped below the beam, acting as one entity, and began the final flight towards the safety of the *Beetle*.

The cannon flashed again, striking down an unlucky elf who hadn't been watching. The luckless soldier exploded into atoms, and was blown away on the wind.

But still, the rest of the group flew forward, striking towards the transport ship like an arrow loosed from a god's bow. Thomas urged himself towards the awaiting ramp of the ship, praying against all hope that they would make it in time.

Suddenly, Thomas' jetpack gave an odd spluttering cough. He jolted in the air, and the flames boosting him forward flickered out, just an arm's length from the ship. Frantically, he pulled the string again, and again, but to no avail.

Desperately, Thomas reached for the metal ramp. His fingers just made contact with the metallic surface, but he simply couldn't get a hold. He began to slide backwards towards the edge and certain death.

Another blast granted him a few more seconds to live. The red laser shot through the ramp, inches from Thomas's fingernails, leaving a smoking, round hole which his outstretched hand managed to find a hold on. He was hanging by two fingers over a fifty thousand foot drop. He was going to die.

Silvanus spun around and saw Thomas' predicament. He cried out, and reached for Thomas' arm. Thomas felt another one of his fingers slip away from his makeshift handhold.

"Take my hand!" shouted Silvanus.

Thomas mustered up the last of his strength and reached with all his might. His splayed fingers met Silvanus' and he found himself being hauled up onto the ship.

Had he waited another second longer, Thomas would have been incinerated by another crimson beam, which shot straight through where his head had been just one moment before.

The ramp lifted up on hidden hydraulics, sealing the opening, and Thomas found himself in a long white room, like the interior of an aeroplane, with rows of seats lining either side. Alex, and at least a dozen more elf soldiers were waiting for him, already strapped into their seats.

Nick sprawled in one of them, out cold and snoring gently, but very much alive. The intensity of the spell had clearly taken its toll on him.

Before Thomas could go to him, a booming voice, enhanced by about 20 speakers, reverberated throughout the room.

"Preparing to accelerate to light speed. Fasten your seatbelts. Entering light speed in T-5... T-4... T-3..."

Thomas dived for his seat.

"T-2..."
He frantically strapped himself in.

"T-1..."

He braced himself.

"0. Entering light speed."

Chapter 5

Raiza

This is the life, thought Raiza. It was a month since Thomas had finally disappeared, and for every single minute of that month, Raiza had thanked whatever God was up there for it over and over again. It was paradise. With the dweeb gone, he could finally rest in peace.

He gazed out of his white-misted window, across the hills to the great white horse, recoloured by the summer sunrise to a fiery red. He was on holiday in Berkshire's 'White Horse Hills', so aptly named after the chalk horse, which had been carved out of the side of the mountain. Some said it was an ancient religious monument, others believed it was a U.F.O. landing runway. Raiza personally didn't care much—he was there for the view. He had been told that just across from the horse was the 'Dragon's Hill' where St. George supposedly slew his dragon. Raiza didn't care about that either.

"Get up, Raiza!"

Raiza's mother was calling. She had said something about a hike the other day, and she probably intended to start now.

"Coming!" he replied, as he rolled off his bed in the White Horseman Hotel. He lazily wandered downstairs, where a quick breakfast and a pair of muddy boots awaited him. Raiza was right—they were hiking.

An hour and a half later, Raiza and his family had nearly reached the top of Dragon's hill. He was wet, tired and wondering if he would ever see anything here other than rocks and shrubs. At last, they reached the foot of a stone flight of steps, carved out of the side of the mound.

As he clambered up them, he noticed that the higher he climbed up the hill, the less vegetation there was. As he pulled himself up onto the top, he found himself on a bare plateau, completely devoid of any signs of life. He walked forward and gazed out across the hills.

He stubbed his toe on something small and black sticking out of the cracked earth. He reached down to it, and gasped as his eyes screamed in pain to look at it. The black was strange; it swam before his vision, almost threatening to draw him inside of it. Resisting the pain, he reached down, gripped it, and pulled. It was stuck fast into the earth. He felt a sudden desire to have it, to hold it in his hand. He grunted, and pulled the black object with all his might. There was an audible *click*, and the thing slid through the earth a few centimetres.

A sharp crack forced him to start forward and almost fall off the sheer ledge. He turned round. Another crack. With a sickening dread he glanced down. The ground was breaking up beneath his feet. Terrified, he started to run forward.

Then the ground completely gave way. With a short scream, Raiza Isingtor began the long plummet towards the core of the hill, and whatever chaos awaited him there.

Raiza awoke in tremendous pain. He sat up, and touched the back of his head with his hand. It came away sticky with blood. He checked his arms and feet, and counted eight cuts and twelve bruises in total. Not bad, considering how far he had fallen. He was lucky to still be alive.

He peered into the blackness. As his eyes adjusted to the gloom, he noticed an unlit old fashioned torch held to a wall in the mouth of a beautifully carved stone dragon. Its wings stretched across the cave wall, and the rubies inside its eye sockets glinted with a devilish light. Something about them stopped him from taking the stones. They held a sort of unspoken command, as if the gems themselves *belonged* there.

He fumbled in his pocket, and brought out the lighter he always carried with him. He clicked it into life, and walked over to the torch - it was full of oil. He held the lighter against the black liquid, and watched as it roared into life.

Pulling it out of the intricately carved stone bracket holding it to the wall, he cautiously walked forward. He cursed as he stumbled on some sort of tree root, weaving its way across the floor. He followed it across the room. It led him to an altar, which appeared to have grown, like a tree, out of the ground. Many more roots twisted out of its wooden base. Glancing around, Raiza noticed seven tall slabs of rock, encircling the altar, each about ten metres from the centre.

Looking around him, he suddenly realised why the setup felt so familiar. Several ridges of rock lined up in neat rows in front of the altar, a thin aisle passing through the middle. The ridges were pews. This whole cave was some sort of church. An unholy church, grown out of the very ground.

"Welcome, mortal..." hissed a voice. Raiza's torch flickered, blown by some ghostly wind, and he spun round. No one was there.

"Don't try to see me, mortal. You can't, unless I let you..." The snake-like voice came again, seeming to surround him, and engulf him.

"Who-who's there?" stuttered Raiza.

"No one. Just me... just the voice in your head."

Voice in his head? Then Raiza understood. Whatever was speaking to him was doing so telepathically, explaining why the voice seemed to resonate from all directions. Either that, or he'd gone insane. It seemed more useful, for now at least, to opt for the former option. "Where am I?"

"You are inside Dragon's Hill. My hill. My home."

"All right. So, how do I get out of here?

"You cannot get out the way you came. Unless you can fly... like I used to..."

"You used to fly?" asked Raiza.

"I used to do many things... but forget that. The only escape is with the altar."

Three coils of twisted stone whipped out from the top of the altar, twisting and dancing around each other before threading themselves into a single object. They knitted together into the form of a small black bowl, resting undisturbed upon the rocky surface, almost as if inviting Raiza to approach. He took a step towards it, and gasped as it began to glow a fiery red.

"Just one drop of blood... Use the knife."

A knife followed the bowl, threading together out of the same impossible strands of stone. It was a long and wicked blade, jagged spikes lining the edge of the fiendish weapon. Raiza suddenly knew what he had to do. He strode over to the bowl, and gripped the black handle.

"That's it. Just one little cut..."

Raiza brought the knife to his arm, and with a wince, pieced the skin. A trickle of hot blood ran down his arm, and he moved it so the liquid dripped into the bowl.

Without warning, the blade twisted in his hand with impossible life, cutting, on its own, all the way through to the bone. Raiza screamed with agony, and collapsed to his knees, but was unable to move either the blade or his wounded hand away from the altar.

The blood continued to pour unchecked into the bowl, filling it right up to the edges, and overflowing, covering the altar in a crimson sea.

"Yes... Just a little more..."

The knife cut deeper, and deeper. With another long, and wolf-like howl, Raiza felt his entire hand disconnect from his arm, and drop with a splash into the bowl. He collapsed to the ground and, suddenly free from the spell, jammed the stump of his wrist under his armpit in a desperate attempt to staunch the flow of blood.

And like the whispering of a wraith in the night, a thousand unseen voices drifted up from the earth below him, joining in an unholy hymn of black triumph. The light drained from Raiza's eyes, blinding him, before sending him falling, falling into a darkness the light of day could never touch.

The speed increase punched Thomas with full force, like Lump and Boil had often done when he had led a normal life.

The ship lurched forward like an enraged animal, and Thomas' head glued itself to the seat headrest, as the G-force took control of his body. Windows on either side of the cabin automatically opened, showing a tremendous view of... absolutely nothing. All outside was black.

Thomas tried to ask why, but he found he couldn't even open his mouth - the force was incredible. He couldn't move. He almost couldn't breathe. He was utterly frozen.

Something went *"Ding!"* and the booming voice came again. "Light speed transition over. You may now move freely. Thank you for choosing Falcon Space Travel. We hope you enjoy your flight."

Thomas unbuckled his seat belt and leapt up.

"Where the heck are we going?" he demanded

"Thomas, Thomas, calm down." replied Nick, "We're just in the middle of a little bit of space travel. I assume this is your first time?"

"No," retaliated Thomas, "back on Earth, I used to zoom around the universe loads. *Of course this is my first time*!"

"Sorry, just checking. A lot could have changed on Earth in the time I was gone. Anyway, right now, we are cruising through Mythicia at over one billion miles per hour – that's much, much faster than the speed of light. You'll feel odd while your body gets used to it. As for the windows, we're moving so fast that your eyes are trying to register millions of galaxies flashing past at the same time. It's too much at once, so your brain gives up, and hence you get black."

"Then what's the point in having windows?" asked Thomas.

Nick ignored him.

Thomas sat back down, and thought. He wished there was something normal, something basic he could grasp hold of, something he could understand. But in this other universe, everything was different, alien. As if answering his prayers, a T.V. screen flipped out of the back of the seat in front of him, flickering into life and displaying an extremely peculiar symbol. It was a circle, divided into four quarters. Each quarter contained a picture with relevance to one of the four elements – Water, Earth, Fire and Air. Then, the word "Elementals" burst into view, written in flaming letters across the monitor.

"What's this?" he asked, baffled.

"It's called a video game." Nick replied, "Don't pretend you don't have them on Earth."

Opal was worried. In fact, she was terrified, but that was something she wouldn't even admit to herself. Thomas had gone, vanished, and she was on her own. She stared up at the blue ceiling, vaguely remembering spending an entire day as a five-year-old choosing the exact shade of pink she had wanted with her mother, only to change her mind to blue at the last minute. There was no way she could sleep, not at a time like this. She climbed out of bed, and wandered downstairs.

The kitchen was cold, and dark, but she flicked the light-switch and the room was filled with a homely yellow glow. She opened the fridge, and poured herself a glass of milk.

She pulled back the curtain, and gazed out at the midnight world. The sight should have made her feel better, she knew, but the normally familiar shapes of her garden seemed distorted in the dark of night. She shivered.

Sipping her milk, she again wondered about her brother. He couldn't have gone voluntarily, that she was certain of. It wasn't in his nature to just leave without telling anyone. He always told Opal everything. He would have known his mother would be worried. Besides, he must have seen the news. *At least he could have phoned*, she thought.

She closed the curtain, and went back to bed. Settling down on the mattress, she wished for her brother.

After a few minutes, she fell asleep, and dreamt of another world.

Thomas grinned. He had just reached the final level of Elementals. He was pitted against the demon lord Demonicus, and he was winning. His health points far exceeded those of the demon, and defeating him should only be a task of hitting the right buttons. But before his fireball could reach Demonicus' chest however, the display went blank. The screen flicked back into the seat, and the seatbelt lights came on.

"What's happening?" he asked "Are we landing?"

"Possibly," Nick replied. "We should be nearing the base by now."

Silvanus' voice boomed out of the hidden speakers, "Looks like we have company. Units three and five to rear cannons, on the double. Units two and four, take side cannons. Unit one, to the cockpit. Passengers, brace yourselves. I'm going to drop out of light-speed. Here we go!"

The voice cut out. Immediately, little flecks of light appeared out the windows. Stars. They were slowing down.

Suddenly, like a ghost forming out of the night, the hideous dark shape of the *Emperor's Wrath* blotted out the tiny pinpricks of light, dominating the blackness of space with its own colossal bulk.

Before the *Wrath* could fire, however, three laser beams erupted from the *Beetle*'s cannons, exploding against the enemy ship and crippling its side. The *Wrath* jolted with the force of the blast. A thin trickle of oily black smoke drifted from the breach in the ship's hull as it turned to face the *Beetle*, and Thomas could see particles of light being drawn towards its main cannon as the laser charged. Silvanus' voice came again.

"Units two and four, open fire in ten seconds, I'm coming round for another pass."

The ship lurched again, and the *Beetle* spun on the spot, it's cannons firing another blast into the *Wrath*'s hull. The force knocked the enemy ship off course, and as its mighty laser fired, the beam passed just to the right of the *Beetle*, missing it by metres.

The laser cannon started to charge again, but this time the *Wrath* swivelled, baring its right flank. Twenty hatches opened in the metal, and from each a small proton missile launched outwards, spiralling towards the *Beetle* like a swarm of angry hornets.

"Unit one, evasive manoeuvres, now!"

The ship ducked and weaved, twisting and darting between the missiles with the grace of a ballet dancer. Its side cannons fired, slicing great swathes through the missiles, but even they could not stop the swarm. At least ten missiles avoided the lasers and hammered into the *Beetle*'s front, and an agonised scream issued from the cockpit.

"Unit one, damage report," Silvanus' voice commanded urgently. Only static returned through the comm. link.

"Repeat, unit one, damage report."

The static crackled and spat, but no voice issued forth.

"Damn it, unit one, come in!"

Still no response.

"Ok, we've lost unit one, I'm assuming manual control myself."

Thomas watched from his seat as Silvanus burst out from one end of the ship and hurried down the aisle, kicking open the door and slipping inside. There was a few moments silence, then Silvanus said: "Unit one's dead. Head smashed in by the proton shockwave."

While this went on, the cannons of the *Beetle* and the *Wrath* still continued to fire, uninterrupted by the goings on inside. The *Wrath* was heavier, stronger, and far more brutal, but the *Beetle* was lighter and more agile, and could avoid the *Wrath*'s attacks without much difficulty. However, when the proton missiles killed the *Beetle*'s pilot, the ship slid to a halt, hanging in space like a sitting target. The *Wrath* lined itself up, targeting the *Beetle* with its central red laser, and began to charge.

"I'm going to enter the atmosphere of the planet below us," Silvanus called down the comm. link. "Hopefully we can lose them in the clouds."

Thomas' stomach lurched as the ship dropped downwards at an alarming speed. Just as he was gathering up the butterflies that had got loose in his stomach, the ship lurched again, only forward. A thundering crack signified the *Wrath* firing its laser and Thomas could swear he'd felt the air tingle as the beam shot past, parting the space above the falling *Beetle* with its terrible power.

Thomas watched through the windows as the starry void transformed into a white blanket of clouds, and then again into a dark blue sky. But glancing away behind the ship, he could see that the *Wrath* was still on their tail. He looked across at Nick, who was clutching the arm rests, his eyes closed, and somehow Thomas knew he was remembering another time. As for Alex, he was staring determinedly out through his window, focused on the *Wrath* and glaring at it with pure unchecked contempt.

In the *Beetle's* cockpit, Silvanus pounded at the controls, pulling the ship through every evasive manoeuvre he could think of. The body of the elf who had been unit one was slumped in the assistant pilot's chair, his broken and bloodied face lolling to one side like a macabre puppet. Silvanus had had to move him, and it hadn't been pleasant.

He had known the elf quite well. His name had been Elethrian, and he had joined Silvanus' squad only a year earlier. He was the youngest of Silvanus' troops, only sixty years of age – barely out of his teens in high elfish culture. Of course, Silvanus was younger, but he had special status in the capital – his mother had been friends with the High Lord, and it hadn't been hard to convince him to allow Silvanus to join up half a decade early.

Silvanus had taken to Elethrian from the start – the elf was an excellent pilot, one of the best Silvanus had ever seen, and he was always sure to keep him in practise. He just hadn't been good enough, it seemed...

Silvanus pulled on a lever, and the ship leapt up into the cloud layer again, darting in and out of the white sheets, always checking back to see the *Wrath* flying lazily not far behind. *They're playing with us*, the elf realised, and he knew all his hope was lost. There was no way they could get away – the *Wrath* was the pinnacle of Magi-tech production; nothing could outrun it, nothing could outfight it.

Silvanus brought the ship round in a wide arc, trying to both hide it amongst the clouds and line it up for an attack. The ship slowed, the *Beetle*'s cannons fired, and surprisingly scored a direct hit on the *Wrath*'s flank. But the mighty vessel only turned, its red laser flared, and Silvanus' face slammed into control desk, stars dancing in his eyes. The ship gave a great metallic groan, and dropped like a stone out of the sky.

Chapter 6

My Name is Valcoz

Sand. It was everywhere, filling Thomas' mouth, eyes, nostrils and ears. Even his throat was thick with the stuff. It was hot and gritty, not the smooth soft stuff one might find on a beach but the rough, grinding skin of the desert. He tried to move, but something heavy and misshapen lay across his back, pinning him down. He was trapped, but at least he was alive.

In an attempt to speak, he opened his mouth, but more thick sand poured down the opening, making him cough and retch, his hot bile mixing with the dust. Suddenly, the onslaught of sand stopped, and he could breathe. He took a long, deep breath of air, lifted his head a fraction, and opened his eyes.

He was still in the ship. He remembered the crash, the flames as he plummeted to what he had thought would be his doom. He had been knocked unconscious, but by some strange twist of fortune it seemed he had managed to avoid being killed. Twisting his neck so that he could peer over his shoulder, the thing that was pinning him down revealed itself to be a huge block of metal – part of the ceiling that had been ripped free as the craft had been crushed into the desert world that they had been flying over when the *Wrath* had hit them.

He strained the muscles across his back and pushed upwards with his legs, hoping to knock the slab off with a single jolt. He felt it move ever so slightly, but as he relaxed it sank back down again, pinning him even tighter than it did before.

Then he heard a voice, calling his name across the sand. He heard the crunch of footsteps, and the scent of crushed pine needles drifted into his nostrils. He felt the great weight shift, and was rewarded with a beam of sunlight, which was almost instantly blotted out by Silvanus' concerned face.

"Thank the gods! You're alive!" he cried.

"Barely," croaked Thomas, coughing up sand and blood with the word, obscuring it until it came out as "Blear". He coughed and retched for a full minute, before he finally had the breath to ask: "What about the others?"

"I think we've rounded up everyone," Silvanus replied, both amused and concerned by Thomas' display. "The ship's emergency protocol kicked in as we were falling – released a gravity bubble to absorb most of the impact. Basically means no one was killed, although you were the last to be found. We'd almost given up hope."

Thomas' momentary surge of relief was extinguished by the realization of just how desolate their situation was.

"Where are we?" he said, pulling himself to his feet.

"Entropia. Turns out we reached our destination after all. Unfortunately, we're on the wrong continent altogether. But we're sending S.O.S signals to anyone in range. Hopefully, the guys at the base will pick it up."

Thomas pulled open the entrance hatch, and gazed out upon the ocean of sand before him. The sun blazed down from an infernal red sky causing the dunes to glisten like a real sea, their ship a lone craft among the shining waves.

Thomas began to walk. Great hills of sand loomed up from a moderately flat, fiery landscape, towering over Thomas' comparatively tiny, insignificant head. It was almost as though they were great tidal waves, frozen in time and turned to dust. Shaking himself, he strode back to the wreck of the ship.

Hurrying along beside him, Silvanus handed him a bottle of clear liquid. Smiling thankfully, he took a long swig from its neck before returning it to the elf. "We haven't got much water," Silvanus began, "so we need to get off this world as soon as possible. We're still transmitting an S.O.S. signal. Anyway, there's no sign of the other ship. Whoever shot us down is long gone. Now, I've assigned a squad to digging for water. There must be some on this wretched planet." The elf turned, and stormed off back to the cockpit.

"Oi! Wake up, ya pest!"

Raiza awoke to strong arms shaking him violently and painfully. As his eyes snapped open, he felt a warm breeze across his forehead. He was lying on dry, yellow straw, in the middle of a wide field. The hands pulled him to his feet, and he stood, looking out at the wide, open farmland surrounding him. He must be back in Berkshire. Unfortunately he had ended up on an angry farmer's land. Just to make sure...

"Wh-Where am I?" he asked, annoyed at himself for stuttering.

"Agricultural area forty-five, Zone fifty-three, planet Berakshirai, GC 4821, 3569. 8712, Mythicia. Now get off me land, ya scum!"

The farmer was very short and very fat, and wore an old chequered flat cap on his head. He had large chubby hands, which still hadn't stopped shaking Raiza, and flecks of black and brown dirt were trapped beneath every fingernail. But the most curious thing about him was his beard. It was tied into a plait, but even so reached all the way down to his knees. It was a fiery ginger, but curiously, the hair on his head was brown.

"Mythicia... what? I thought I was in Berkshire!" exclaimed Raiza

"Sorry, but I don't know of any Berkshire 'roud 'ere. What GC is it, lad?"

"What's a GC? A games console?"

"Great Thor, where did ya go to school? Galactic Coordinates, ya dunce!"

"What?" Raiza said, bemused. "*Galactic* coordinates? You're saying I'm not even on Earth anymore?"

"Ach, ya really 'ave lost it mate! Earth? You're livin' in an 'uman tale, elf. Mind you, what 'appened to ya ears?"

"What's wrong with my ears?" Raiza was confused beyond comprehension. "I'm not an elf! I'm human, completely and utterly. What else could I be?"

"Ha!" laughed the farmer. "You, an 'uman? No chance, mate. Now, I like ya, so I'll give ya a chance. I'm gonna walk away, and when I come back in ten minutes and you ain't still 'ere, I'll forget this ever 'appened, OK?" He turned and started walking away.

"Wait!" called Raiza.

"Go away or I'll call the Intercops!"

Raiza understood that. The 'Intercops' were clearly this place's 'Police'. He turned, and suddenly had an idea. He fumbled in his pocket. *I hope it didn't break in my fall,* he thought.

He brought out his mobile and began to dial...

Damn!

Raiza couldn't get a signal. Wherever he was, clearly it wasn't Berkshire. Berkshire had a great signal. He threw down his mobile and started to walk.

As he walked, he thought of what had happened to him. He had been enjoying (well… sort of) a sunny walk in Berkshire, he had fallen into a hole, been tricked into cutting his own hand off, and kicked off a farm. Wait! His hand! He glanced down at his wrist. His hand was there, as real as ever, though. He must have been dreaming. But that didn't explain where he was. He was so confused, and focussed on trying to work it all out, he had stopped watching where he was going, and didn't notice the man cross his path, before he crashed straight into him, and thudded to the floor. He lay there, dazed for a moment. Suddenly, a hand was reaching towards him. Raiza thankfully took it, and was pulled to his feet.

"Sorry," began Raiza.

"Don't apologise," replied the stranger, "'twas my fault really. Should 'ave been lookin' where I was goin'."

Raiza found himself looking at another farmer, who was also very short, with another long beard. He had a look of kindly concern on his face.

"Name's Grollim. I own this 'ere plot of land. You an elf then?"

"No," groaned Raiza, "I'm a human. I'm lost, and everyone keeps calling me an elf. I just want to go home!"

"All right lad. Where's 'ome then? D'ya know its GC?"

"No, I'm from Earth, and I need to get back to Berkshire!"

"Earth?" chortled the farmer, "Surely not *the* Earth? You ain't an 'uman? That's mad!"

"No, seriously, I'm human. Just take a look at me!" Raiza was getting frustrated.

"Mate, it ain't All Hallow's Eve or April Fools, so today really ain't the time to play around. I'm a busy dwarf."

"I swear I'm telling the truth! Believe me! Please!"

"...All right then. Ya seem like a nice enough lad, so I'll tell ya what. Come with me to the mage's 'ouse, and 'e'll tell us the truth."

A voice Raiza knew all too well began to sound in his head.

Do what he says. Go with him, or you'll be lost forever.

The return of the voice filled Raiza with dread.

Raiza followed Grollim back across the fields, and into a sort of campsite. Two rows of small leather tents lined the edges of the camp, and a far larger, square tent with an entrance of stringed beads stood in the middle. As he passed the first tent, two tall, hooded, black-clad figures emerged from nowhere and blocked their path.

"What brings you to the camp before your designated work-time is up, Farmer Grollim?" one hissed in a voice that sucked the warmth from the air.

"This boy showed up on my land," Grollim said firmly. "I'm taking 'im to see the mage."

"You will return to your duties, Grollim," the other figure whispered. "The Throne of Bones does not tolerate unscheduled breaks."

"Let them pass, demon!" a voice called from inside the larger tent.

Both figures hissed in anger, but stepped aside. Raiza and Grollim continued towards the tent, eyeing the black-clad men as they passed.

Grollim brushed aside the beads that hung from the entrance-flap, and pushed Thomas forward into the tent. Inside sat a withered old man dressed in dirty black robes, staring into a green glass ball that was positioned on a round table.

"Sit down, child," said the mage. The man's voice was old and creaky. That was the only way Raiza could describe it. It sounded just like an old and rusty door being pushed open. The man's face was so covered in lines and wrinkles that it seemed as if his head was a deflated football, sitting atop a pair of sagging shoulders. The only things sharp about him were his ears, which were at least four inches long, and pointed like daggers.

"I've come to-" began Raiza, but the mage cut him off.

"I know why you're here." He creaked. "You wish to prove your race to the dwarf. You wish to make him see that you are a human. You wish for me to tell him it is so." He turned to Grollim. "He is human, short one. You may leave him in my care; I will keep him from harm."

The dwarf muttered something about speciesism under his breath, turned, and almost sprinted out.

"Child," began the mage.

"My name's Raiza!"

"Very well. How old would you say I am, Raiza?"

Raiza felt awkward. He didn't want to insult the man, but he didn't want to lie either. "Eighty?" He guessed. Even then he was guessing younger than he thought the man was.

"I am thirty-five." The man replied with a toothless smile.

"What? You're joking!"

"It is true I am a mage. I use magic. But I am not that old. Have you ever heard of glamour magic?"

Finally, something Raiza knew. He had read about glamour magic in a fantasy fiction book, "It's in stories, fantasy books, like when you change what you look like with magic?"

"Magic is most certainly not a story. And you've just been talking to a dwarf. Anyway, you were right about glamour. I am using it now. Watch."

Suddenly, the withered old man began to grow taller. The wrinkles smoothed themselves out, the gnarled hands elongated, and the nails became a healthy peach. The withered old man was gone, and in his place stood a tall, handsome man. Only the eyes stayed the same – a bright green, just like Raiza's.

"My name is Valcoz. Unlike you, however I am an elf. A low elf, to be precise, not that it matters to you."

"You-you changed?" Raiza gasped.

"Correct. It's called magic, Raiza. And I want to teach it to you."

"You want to teach me magic? You've only just met me!"

"Oh, I've known you for a long time. I've watched you since your birth. One day I'll tell you how... but today you must come with me." Valcoz stood up and made for the door.

"Wait!" Raiza stopped him "How do I know I can trust you?"

"You don't have to trust me, just come!"

"I've got enough sense not to go with people I've never met. How do I know you're not going to just knife me or something?"

Valcoz turned, and Raiza noticed his eyes had developed red flecks in the centre of each pupil, "*Come!*"

Raiza tried to speak, to say no, but he found he couldn't open his mouth – he couldn't move at all. Then, he felt his legs move. He found himself walking towards Valcoz. His legs were moving of their own accord. He was a prisoner in his own body.

Chapter 7

Contact

We've made contact!"

The shout raised Thomas from his deep sleep. "What?" he asked, drowsily rolling off his makeshift mattress.

"We've made contact!" Silvanus called again, "Someone's picked up our signal!"

Thomas leapt up this time, instantly alert. "Rebels?"

"It's too early to tell. Come here!" Thomas climbed out of the cave that the team had dug into the sand the night before, and strode over to the wrecked ship. The main computer was still working, and it was here that Silvanus was sitting, poised over the glowing square screen. Coming from the speakers were long periods of static, with the occasional crackle of distorted speech.

"They're on the other side of the planet- the signal's broken up; they need to come round. The radar's broken, so I can't find out how many ships there are, or indeed what they are. But they seem friendly enough."

Another crackle from the speakers cut him off. A deep, barely audible voice began to make itself heard.

"What is your GC? Over!" They both stared at the speaker. "Repeat, what is your GC? Over!"

Silvanus leapt into action, almost shattering the computer's touch screen with the force of his finger scrolling through endless numbers and codes. He seemed to find what he was looking for, and read it out into a small microphone sticking out the keyboard. "GC 4513, 1202, 3435. Over!"

"Copy that. Navigating now. Over!" came the reply.

Silvanus grinned. "They're coming to save us! We're being rescued!" he cried, grinning.

As he and Thomas flailed around, laughing and crying and dancing with happiness, Thomas accidentally slammed his fist into the side of the computer. The screen flickered, then died. Silvanus' laughter cut off when he saw the screen. He desperately hammered at the keyboard, pounding the keys like an animal. After a few moments, the screen burst back into life.

"The radar!" Silvanus cried, "Don't ask me how, but you've fixed it! Look, whilst it warms up, I'll show you the key! See. It's really a very clever system. The biosensitive engineering allows the radar to identify what type of creature pilots the craft. For example, if the dot indicating the ship is green, it's friendly. If it's red, it's a demon. Let's flick back to the main screen, the radar should have warmed up by now. Notice how the dots representing the ships who intercepted our signal are green..." he trailed off, as red dots filled the screen. They were not being rescued. They were being destroyed.

Raiza felt himself walk out of the tent and away. Following Valcoz, his body rebelled against Raiza's every command. The feeling of your body moving without your control was terrifying, like some strange obscure nightmare. Raiza felt each muscle tense, and each limb lift and move, as though he was being pulled by strings that were not only invisible, but *weren't even there.* He felt the crunch of the gravelly track beneath his boots, and smelt the fresh country air with every breath, but even his breathing was under the mage's control. It was slow, and shallow; Raiza was only getting just enough air to stay conscious.

Raiza could only watch as he left the campsite and strode down the worn track towards the edge of a dark, brooding collection of vaguely normal trees. If he wasn't on Earth, he was certainly somewhere like it. Even the sun and the sky looked the same. As they entered the wood, the crunch of the track shifting to the rustle of fallen leaves, Valcoz stopped.

"Portide Gumethotheal," the elf hissed in a language Raiza couldn't recognise.

Suddenly, a glowing orb of light materialised by Valcoz's shoulder. It floated forward, pulsing occasionally. Valcoz followed it, and Raiza was forced to go with him. The orb danced and twirled through the trees, ducking and weaving under the branches and bracken, Valcoz following all the time. Eventually, the orb led them into a circular forest clearing, ringed by an odd circle of stones, arranged just like Stonehenge. The dancing light came to rest in the centre of the clearing, and Valcoz strode right after it, Raiza staggering along behind him. As they neared the centre, the orb shattered into fragments of light, dissolving into the air like a ghost.

"We're here." Valcoz murmured coldly.

He stepped into the circle, and vanished. Raiza began to panic. He tried to turn back, to hurl himself away, but he could not. Despite Valcoz's absence, his own body still refused to obey him. He screamed silently as he unwillingly walked into the circle himself.

Light. That was all Raiza saw. Streams of colour washed around him as he fell through a never-ending void of confusion and fear. Reds and blues and greens sliced across his mind, and his eyes burned with an alien fire as he was hurled uncontrollably about the vortex.

He screamed with both exhilaration and pain, flying through the madness, soaring through a tide of whirling insanity. Nothing mattered here. He was at one with the essence of chaos itself.

As he fell through the twisting light, the distant colours seemed to form into a distinguishable shape. In fact, he could have sworn it was a tree. As he squinted into the madness, a deep resounding voice echoed through his brain.

"The Fall and the Destined, a broken lord.

The Destined's blade, an Ancient's sword.

The Fall will be felled, the tears will restore.

The end will draw near, as it happened before.

In the Black Star's shadow, in the circle of stones,

The Fall and the Destined, before the Throne of Bones,

Can release the Old Darkness, and break the last seal,

And all of Creation before the Dragon shall kneel."

And then it was over.

The light flashed out of existence, and Raiza fell to an iron floor, banging his head on the metal. Unable to stand, he felt around the ground with his fingers, trying to grasp hold of something, anything. His mind still rang with the echoes of the voice, and the light of the colours blazed on the back of his eyelids. Slowly, ever so slowly, he forced his eyes to open, and stared at the silver panel pressed right against his face.

Raiza pushed down with his feet, and heaved himself upright, bemused to find himself standing on a rectangular iron platform, impossibly floating above an incomprehensibly vast wasteland, stretching beyond the horizon and probably many miles further.

Nothing grew upon the stricken plains; only a few withered plant corpses lingered on the bronze dust where all other life had passed. Raiza felt a hand upon his shoulder as he gazed across the wreckage. He looked up at Valcoz, who was scrutinising him like a scientist inspecting a specimen before dissection. Ringing the platform's edges was a circle of metal pillars, uncannily similar to the stone circle Raiza had entered just minutes before.

"Where are we?" asked Raiza.

"You are at the site of the Last of the Demon Wars. You are in Mythicia – a universe parallel to your own, where only monsters exist and humans are legendary. Mythicia is ruled by the demons." Valcoz spoke quickly, but a bored expression carpeted his face. It was if he was reciting from a script he had performed millions of times before.

"This is where they defeated the United Races - Elves and suchlike." Valcoz continued. "Those of the defeated Unity have formed a rebel alliance, but they have little hope. I work for whoever pays me most, and that is currently the Demon Empire. You will be my apprentice. It is true I am a mage, but I am also a necromancer. That means-"

Raiza cut him off, surprised to find he was keeping up with everything Valcoz was saying. He knew what "necromancer" meant as well. "-You raise the dead."

"Correct, apprentice. And you will learn to be one too – whether you want to or not."

"But that's impossible! What's dead stays dead." Raiza protested. He was still having trouble with the concept of another universe full of demons and monsters, and the idea of being able to resurrect the fallen made his head feel fit to explode.

"Really?" Valcoz said with a smile. "Then why can I do this?" The necromancer raised his hand, his fingers hanging downwards like the strings of a puppet.

Below, in the barren wasteland, a white skeletal hand burst from the soil. It pressed against the dusty ground, and was soon followed by an arm, then another hand. Slowly and awkwardly, a complete skeleton pulled itself out of the earth, in a full Roman suit of armour, a murky brown skull grinning maliciously out of an age old helmet. It slammed its forearm against its chest in an ancient salute.

"No..." Raiza was lost for words, "Way cool..." he breathed.

"Yes, very cool. Icy, even. And you shall be able to do that and much more very soon... Just listen to my words, and be patient. Now, let's start with a simple spell, like raising the weakest of creatures such as rabbits..."

Chapter 8

The Prophecy

Silvanus charged into the cave where Nick, Alex and the elven troopers were desperately trying to keep cool, Thomas following close behind. "Demons!" Silvanus yelled. "They've found us. They tricked us into giving them our GC. We don't have much time. All units! Mobilize!"

Instantaneously, the elf troopers leapt to their feet. Within a minute, they were in full armour, machine guns at the ready. Nick and Alex were not so quick to respond. The elderly mage slept right on through Silvanus' warning, and Alex took a moment to realise exactly what was going on. The blonde boy rolled off his log and placed his helmet back on to his head, drawing his knife as he did so. He laid a hand on his master's shoulder, and shook him until he woke.

The mage groaned, and staggered to his feet. He brushed down his robes, and together he, Alex and Thomas stood with Silvanus' elves, waiting for the approaching conflict. Nick whipped his staff out from beneath his robes, and extending it to its full length, pushed it into the ground beside him. Thomas drew his sword, and held it out in front of him, his eyes fixed on the entrance to the cave.

BANG! The earth shook, and the edges of the cave's ceiling collapsed in a rain of dust and shattered rock. "They're here!" Silvanus cried, lifting his weapon.

A dozen demons poured through the hole, screeching and shouting, all trying to be the first to draw blood. Each was of a different size and shape, some horned, some with tails, and some even with wings like a bat's. They screeched and called, pouring forward like a living tide, biting and scratching and lashing out with their tails. The elves planted their feet into the sand and opened fire, shattering the demonic sea with bolts of fiery plasma. Demons screamed and roared, many toppling like dominoes onto the rocky floor. But still, the tide continued, more and more raging demons replacing their fallen, some even devouring their dead kin.

The elves fired again, and again, felling even more and more of the monsters, but nothing could halt the onslaught. The line of demons stretched closer and closer to the defendants, and soon it would be upon them.

"Hitomas nelethelia!" Nick roared slamming his hands against the tip of his staff, and seizing it from its planted position. He whirled it above his head, and a long coiled whip of flame streamed from the pole, and he allowed it trail behind his back. With an angry shout, he swiped the staff forward and down, pulling the stream of fire with it and hammering it down into the demon ranks. At least twenty demons fell beneath the flaming whip, and as Nick moved the staff left and right the fire lashed from side to side, striking down demon after demon, cutting a great swathe through the monstrous ranks.

Thomas and Alex stood on either side of the mage, slicing and stabbing with their blades at any demon who got close. Nick was the most important weapon, and as long as his spell wasn't interrupted, he could hold the demons off. And so it was that Thomas was so focused on protecting the mage that he never saw the black horned imp hanging from the ceiling above him, and could not lift his blade in time to stop it from dropping down onto Nick and sinking its teeth into the mage's shoulder.

The great whip of fire evaporated instantly, the staff fell from Nick's hands, and the mage collapsed under the infernal imp. Alex turned, horror etched across his face, and he drove his knife into the demon's back, but too late. Even as it fell dead to the ground, Nick lay twitching in a crimson pool of his own blood, his face a mask of terror and pain.

Alex began to murmur in True Speak, caressing the wounded mage, "Go on, help hold the line," he told Thomas between verses. "I need time to heal him." Thomas nodded, and he ran back to join Silvanus and the elves.

Many of the demons had been killed by Nick's spell, so the cave was relatively clear compared to how it had been moments before. Only one or two demons came through the opening every ten seconds now, and most were picked off by the plasma rifles before they could make a move towards the defendants.

"Don't start to relax, boys!" Silvanus called to his soldiers. "There's no way they'd give up this quickly!"

And sure enough, even as the flow of demons dwindled near to a halt, a great wave of the creatures burst through the opening like a plug had been pulled, and amongst the hundreds of creatures was a monster from Thomas' worst nightmares.

It was twice the height of a human; so tall, it had to stoop to fit into the cave. Its pale blue skin shone in the light as it staggered forward with a lumbering gait. It looked in most respects like a giant human, but only a single eye pulsed in the centre of its forehead, where two would normally sit. The eye was red and bloodshot, but above all, it was fixed on Thomas.

It had to be a cyclops. Thomas had read about them back home on Earth. One featured in Homer's *Odyssey*, Polyphemus. It had been described almost exactly like this one, just not so blue, and not quite so terrifying.

Silvanus raised his hand, and the elves charged at the approaching demons, firing madly. Most of the demons collapsed, but the gaps were soon filled by another wave of the creatures pouring into the cave, each just as eager to kill as their predecessors. The great cyclops roared, pulling at the iron chains that stretched from each of its limbs, binding it to four separate guard demons, but the bullets seemed only to anger the creature. Alex pulled Nick to his feet, and Nick yelled and raised his staff, his shoulder wound healed by Alex's magic. A spear of white light shot from its tip, blasting a swathe of demons from his path. Alex drew his knife, and started to hack at the approaching onslaught, felling everything that was unlucky enough to face him.

The cyclops burst through the lines of demons, and was on the defenders like a maddened wolf. It swung a boulder-sized fist, knocking the elves down like matchsticks. It stamped and shouted, and the unfortunate demons trying to bring it under control were hurled across the cave as their chains snapped.

Alex somersaulted through the air, and landed at the cyclops' feet. With a great battle cry, he drove his knife deep into the creature's shin. It screamed, a terrible, fearsome sound, and the stench of bad blood poured from the wound. The giant's eye pulsed, and he swatted Alex away like a fly. He flew through the air and crashed against a jagged rock wall, where he slumped, unconscious.

Thomas stared after his friend, and took a step towards him, to help him, but stopped and faced the cyclops instead. He had to kill it first, before it could do any more damage, and then he would have time to help Alex. Thomas ignited his sword and made a charge at the cyclops. He hacked and slashed at the demons surrounding it, sweeping towards the giant with all the speed his rage could grant him. The mighty creature turned, and stared at him with its single eye, as if to judge how much of a threat he presented. It growled through its murky brown teeth, and brought its fist down towards Thomas' head.

Thomas leapt to one side, rolling across the floor before springing to his feet. He glanced at the crater the impact of the giant's fist had made in the floor, and winced. If he were hit, it would most certainly hurt.

He made another run at the titanic creature. It swung another fist in a sweeping strike, attempting to knock Thomas off his feet. In a sudden moment of inspiration, Thomas jumped up and grabbed a hold on the tree-trunk arm, digging his fingers into its blue flesh. He scrambled up the limb as if it were a ladder and crouched on the cyclops' shoulder, wrapping his arms around its head and swaying as the monster charged around the cave, trampling demons and elves alike. Roaring as it stopped, it lifted a hand to swat Thomas off.

The hand never even came close. Thomas buried his sword in the cyclops' neck in a wide swing, and with a sickening jerk, the head tumbled to the floor. Thomas whooped in triumph, but his jubilations soon turned to screams as the cyclops' body toppled to the floor, pinning him beneath its limp form.

Thomas started to panic. He couldn't move, he could barely even breathe. The titanic corpse was crushing him against the floor like a great fleshy vice– it was all Thomas could do to retain his consciousness. He screamed again, but the blue body lay across his face, and the sound caught in its muscular rolls.

And then he felt a pair of strong hands on his shoulders, and he was pulled from under the fallen cyclops, his sword sliding smoothly out of the creature's bloodied neck. Thomas looked up at his rescuer. It was one of Silvanus' elves.

"Are you all right?" the elf asked. "I'm fine," Thomas replied. "Just had a bit of a fright there." The elf's eyes widened in horror as a muticle rose up behind Thomas, malevolent intent burning deep within its eye. The bloodshot pupil glowed momentarily, and it let fly its burning stream. The elf rammed into Thomas, knocking him to the floor, and a bolt of pain lanced through his leg as he felt his ankle crack. He screamed, but the elf screamed louder as the creature's eye fired a concentrated beam of fire straight through his brain, creating a neat hole in the centre of his forehead. Thomas leapt to his feet, slicing the muticle into two halves.

The creature collapsed to the cave floor, and Thomas turned and knelt by the fallen elf's side. He felt his rescuer's pulse, but he knew it was hopeless. The elf was dead, and he had died saving Thomas. It wasn't fair. How could life be extinguished so easily? And how did the demons have the right to deal death in such a fiendish manner? He dragged the elf's corpse to the back of the cave, and returned to the fight.

The skeleton crumbled away. "Damn!" cursed Raiza, after failing his twentieth try.

"Fret not, apprentice, you shall gain the skill eventually," replied Valcoz, "I've practised the art of necromancy for longer than you've been alive. Now focus. Again!"

Raiza sighed, and raised his hands. "Sufemeron cefor!" he cried.

The silent wasteland remained as still as a corpse, the few dead plants untouched by the light breeze's fingers. Raiza clenched his teeth as he waited, hoping against hope that the spell had worked.

And then, to his surprise and satisfaction, something small and white leapt out of the cracked earth. It scampered toward the floating platform, where it paused, and looked up, expectantly. It was the animated skeleton of a rabbit.

"Wow..." breathed Raiza.

"Well?" persisted Valcoz, raising an eyebrow. "Go on, command it!"

Raiza smiled. "*Come*!" he commanded.

The rabbit leapt straight into the air, almost as if it were flying, and landed on the platform at Raiza's side. It stopped, and looked up at him again.

"Tell it to do something useful," said Valcoz

"All right. *Find me food!*" The rabbit leapt down from the platform, and disappeared into the distance.

"Excellent," said Valcoz, "A little crude perhaps, but effective nonetheless. Let's try something more complicated. Think about a *person*."

"A person?" asked Raiza, astonished. He wasn't sure he wanted to raise a person.

"Yes. You don't think you can defend the Empire with an army of rabbits, do you? You saw what I did earlier. Concentrate!"

Raiza, if a little, hesitantly, took a step forward, and raised his hands. He looked at Valcoz.

"Go on," the necromancer insisted.

"Sufemeron cefor!"

The ground parted beneath the platform, creating an enormous fissure, slicing the land in two. Out of the fissure, on a rocky pillar, rose a greenish-blue hunched figure. It wasn't a skeleton. But it wasn't a man either.

"A half-life…" muttered Valcoz.

"A half-life?" repeated Raiza.

"Yes. Or, to use the colloquial term, a zombie."

The zombie raised its head, looking up at Raiza with red, soulless eyes. There was no pupil, no iris of any kind, simply just a red ball, fixed in a decaying socket.

"You get them now and again," explained Valcoz. "When you're tired, or scared, that sort of thing. You're squeamish. You feel bad about raising a real person."

"You're right," replied Raiza, "I can't quite bring myself to do it. I couldn't focus."

"To be a necromancer, you must learn to abandon all emotions. You must forget your past life. You must become cold and immune to the illusions of morality. Ah. It appears your rabbit's back."

The thing that used to be a rabbit scampered towards the platform, clutching something brown in its mouth. It took another unearthly leap, and landed at Raiza's feet. It dropped the brown thing at Raiza's feet. He bent down and picked it up. It squirmed in his hand.

Raiza yelped in disgust and dropped the worm. "But I told it to bring me food!" he exclaimed.

"You weren't specific. There are millions upon millions of things in Mythicia that would fit the definition of "food." It brought you *its idea* of food. When it was alive it ate that sort of thing. Thus it brought you what it thought you would like. When you use necromancy, you must be *absolutely* specific when giving commands. Otherwise your minions will mess things up. Now thank it and dismiss it."

"Err… thank you? And umm… you can go now."

The rabbit crumbled away into a heap of bones.

Thomas left the limp body of the elf on the floor. There was no time for a proper burial. He felt the rage build up inside him. He felt it coursing through his veins, igniting his heart. He was dimly aware of himself rising up into the air, but through the red mist of his anger, he didn't feel the need to question it. He roared, and raised his hands.

Lightning shot from his fingertips, forking out across the cave. Nick, Alex and the defending elves scattered and dived for cover, the crackling energy lashing in every direction. He felt as if he were burning up from the inside - flames seared away from his whole body, lashing the walls.

"I am the Destined," he shouted, and a thousand whispers accompanied the words, filling them with dark and terrifying power.

"I am the Destined, and you do not belong here." Thomas roared again, and the force of a millennia's magic flared from his form and out, piercing the hearts of every howling and screeching demon in the room. Each let loose an ear-piercing scream, their lamentations joining in a soul-rending chorus of torment. And then, each and every one of them crumbled to dust. No sooner had this happened, Thomas felt himself flying forward, and out, out of the cave, and over the sand.

His wild eyes glared at the world around him, at the beauty of the dunes stretching out into eternity, at the beauty of the sun glittering off the shining sands. And then he looked up, up at the ugliness of the *Emperor's Wrath*, squatting against the otherwise flawless skyline.

Thomas' eyes narrowed into slits, and he rose upwards towards the *Wrath*, blazing with fire and energy. The ship's guns and cannons swivelled towards him, letting a volley of missiles and plasma bolts soar down at the approaching boy. The firepower would have been enough to take down a ship, and should have utterly obliterated Thomas' lone form. Should have done, but didn't.

Thomas whispered a string of True Speak, and the fires blazed brighter, lashing out around him and burning the projectiles to ashes.

The missiles collapsed to blackened dust, the plasma bolts winked out of existence, and Thomas simply gained speed as his anger built, his hands reaching out for the *Wrath* with deadly intent.

Within seconds he was floating just beneath the *Wrath*, and he stared at it with contempt for a moment. Then, he pounded a flaming fist into the ship's hull; blue-green cracks spiralled out from his strike, branching in all directions across the black metalwork.

Next, he placed a single finger on the cracked surface, and the entire ship shattered into shards, exploding in a ball of smoke and flame. He drifted away from the broken spaceship, and watched as it fell to pieces in front of him.

And then, the power left him. He fell to the floor. For how long he lay there, weeping into the desert's sand, none could say, but to Thomas it felt like an eternity. And then, the sound of feet padding across the hot earth reached his ears, and he felt strong hands taking hold of his shoulders, and lifting him to his feet. Nick had followed him away from the cave, and allowed Thomas to lean on him for support.

"That was incredible," the mage murmured his voice filled with awe. "So much power. How can one person control that colossal strength?"

"I didn't," Thomas panted, frowning, suddenly scared. "It controlled me."

"What do you mean?" asked Nick, incredulous. "You just single handedly killed an entire demon attack force, flagship and all."

"When the power came over me," Thomas breathed, "I didn't know what I was doing. I couldn't control myself. I was so angry. I wanted to destroy them all for what they did to that elf. He saved my life!"

"Ah," replied Nick. "That's not good." He paused, rolling thoughts round in his head. "I think you could well have just suffered from a fairly strong case of Bloodrage."

"Bloodrage?"

"Bloodrage. It's an interesting phenomenon that occurs when a magic user gives in to their anger. Their powers increase to their full potential, and all their potential Disciplines are made available to them, but they frequently lose control. It takes a lot of self discipline to control Bloodrage. Still, yours certainly demonstrated immensely powerful magic. You're incredibly strong."

"Great," Thomas replied. This was too much. How could he be the wielder of such powerful magic? And what was the point of having it if he couldn't control it?

"Then I don't want it," he concluded.

Nick stared at him for a few seconds. "What?"

"If my magic's going to do that much damage, and I can't control it when I'm angry, I don't want it."

Nick's mouth hung open like a goldfish.

"I'm serious," Thomas continued. "One day I might hurt someone."

"I suppose that's true," Nick admitted. "But there are... ways... of suppressing Bloodrage. I suppose, if you really wanted me to, I could help suppress the magic. I have to warn you though, if we go through with this, you won't be able to access your magic so easily when you're angry."

"It's what I want," Thomas said, determinedly.

"Right then," the mage replied, clapping his hands together. We'll get started as soon as we have a spare moment."

"Why me?" Thomas interrupted.

"What?"

"Why do I have such powerful magic? Surely it would be better with someone like you."

Nick gave a long, wistful sigh. "Because I'm not the Destined. There's a prophecy amongst the rebels. It's centuries old, but it has never come true. It goes like this:

The darkness returns,

The galaxy burns.

The Destined spreads light,

Behold his might.

As the heart beats faster,

The shadow is master.

The demon legacy shall crumble to dust,

The Calling shall sound and awaken black lust,

Revealing the truth of the empty Throne,

The old darkness rises to make it its own.

The Destined shall ride as the Dragon grows strong,

One must fall for the right or the wrong."

"How does that explain why I have such powerful magic?" Thomas asked.

"Well," Nick replied, "Your sword is inscribed 'For the Destined' so 'The Destined' must be you. So maybe you've been chosen to have this power to try and stop this 'Shadow', which is probably Malcaractimus. As for the 'Dragon', who can say?"

"How do you know?"

"I've seen prophecies before. They're so predictable."

"You mean that someone, a very long time ago, actually knew that all this would happen, and wrote it down?"

"No," the mage replied, "but it's a lie that works."

"So, I'm supposed to defeat this "Shadow"?"

"Yes."

"And I have more power than any of the other magi in Mythicia?"

"Yes."

"Sweet!"

"Sufemeron cefor!" Raiza commanded, raising his arms.

The earth shook, a great chasm opened in the ground, and five pale half-lifes rose from the ground upon one stone pillar. Valcoz clapped his bony hands, slowly and carefully.

"Well done..." he said, and a hint of emotion crossed his face. "It seems you are ready for your first task. I have received word from our demon masters. They require a necromancer to... remove... a mage known as Elthorn the Turbulent. However, it appears I have an errand to attend to. Thus, I cannot go, so I am sending my apprentice instead. That's you," he added, as Raiza looked around in surprise.

"The mage is powerful, but he's nothing you can't handle. Now, step into the stone circle we came through, and you should emerge at the Nel'craz circle, about a kilometre from where the mage lives. He's a hermit, so don't expect to find a town."

Raiza nodded, and Valcoz placed his hands on one of the pillars ringing the platform. "Ilcasimo portide num Nel'craz voe silathreal," he commanded, and a deep purple globe of light the height of a man shimmered into existence at the centre of the circle. The necromancer inclined his head towards the sphere, and Raiza hesitated. "Go on!" insisted Valcoz, placing a hand on Raiza's shoulder. "Prove your worth to me!"

Raiza took a deep breath, and stepped into the light.

Chapter 9

Worms

The oddly assorted troupe of rebels continued their trek across the sands. Silvanus had decided against returning to the ship, reasoning that the demons knew of its location, and reinforcements could well be lying in wait. So they had little choice but to walk onward in the general direction of the base they'd originally been headed for, in the hope they came across a settlement of some kind. It was a slim chance, but the only one they really had.

It was on the second day of their trek, living off only the meagre rations they had recovered from the *Beetle,* that Thomas asked Nick a question that had been niggling at him for a while. "Why English?"

"I beg your pardon?" Nick replied, slowing his pace.

"Everyone we've met so far since I left Earth speaks English. Why?"

Nick stared at Thomas for a few moments. "I have absolutely no idea," he said, slowly. "To be totally honest with you, it's not something that's occurred to me before. We don't call it English, to us, its New Elfish – the language the elves devised after True Speak became empowered. Given the elves' passion for travel, it's only natural that now most of the universe speaks it. I'll give it-"

He stopped, as Alex cried out. "The sea! I can see water!"

The group broke into a headlong sprint towards the distant streak of blue. Thomas was one of the first to reach it, and hurled himself armour and all into the cool waves, allowing them to wash away the sand and sweat that had plagued his body since he had first left the ship. Alex whooped and dived in after him, and before long, the two of them were laughing and splashing together as carefree as infants. Nick called them over with a shout.

"Lady Luck has been kind to us – we have found water!" He dipped his index finger into the waves and tasted it. "The water is clean. Which means we can drink it. No salt, no nothing. Surprising. All the same, water does not only mean drink – it will also bring us fish. We shall dine on seafood tonight!"

Several things then happened at once. Alex and Thomas high-fived. The earth shook. One of Silvanus' elves vanished. And finally, a colossal, spiked worm-like creature erupted from the sand behind Nick.

It was long and brown, the only thing on its head being an enormous round maw, through which one could see down in its throat and, if one looked closer (which really wouldn't be a good idea), into its stomach. The opening was lined with several rows of jagged teeth, rotating like some giant, horrific shredder. The teeth dripped with fresh blood, with a few locks of elf-like silver hair caught between them. Time seemed to stand still as the hideous creature loomed over them. Then, the spell was broken by the chatter of machine gun fire, as the remains of Silvanus' elves started shooting madly at the creature, which responded with an unearthly scream, before falling upon the brave warriors.

Many an elf had their machine guns ripped away from them, and were then themselves crushed into their next life between the creature's grinding teeth. It attacked without hesitation, randomly moving from one target to the next, engulfing all in its terrifying onslaught. Then, as suddenly as the creature had appeared, it vanished into the sand.

"What the..." murmured Silvanus

"A medusa worm... fascinating." breathed Nick

"How can you say that?" Thomas asked, astounded. "That thing just slaughtered half of Silvanus' elves, and all you can do is be fascinated?

What is a medusa worm anyway?”

“Look, Thomas,” replied Nick, “I’m a scientist and a mage. It’s my job to be fascinated. If I weren’t, then no one would ever learn anything about any creature that ever killed sentient life. But to answer your question, medusa worms live on desert planets like this one. They’re naturally carnivores, and will eat practically anything that moves. Unfortunately, that includes us.”

“Where did it go?”

“To get the rest of its pack.” Nick replied grimly.

Upon hearing this, the rest of the group ran straight for the shoreline, throwing nervous glances in all directions as they moved.

“Hey!” an elf shouted, “I can see something!”

Sure enough, something tall and brown could be seen poking over the edge of a distant dune. Was it another worm? No. It was a wooden pole, with a large white sheet hanging off one side

“I think it’s a mast!” called out Alex.

Sure enough, as they got closer to the mast, it revealed itself to be attached to a white cloth. As they drew closer, the white cloth revealed itself as a sail, and the sail was attached to a ship. Thomas never had time to ponder how it had got there, however, because the moment they took a step towards the boat, a long, brown, twisting creature burst from a far-away dune. The medusa worm was indeed back with its pack. And they were hungry.

Raiza emerged from the portal straight into a swamp. The moment he had stopped falling through space and appeared in this murky wasteland, he had smelt a stench so powerful it had made his nostrils burn.

"Where the devil am I now?" he asked.

A sort of toad hopped out of the slimy waters and rubbed against Raiza's leg. Repulsed, he kicked it away. It let loose a miserable squeal, and rolled over, revealing an extra pair of legs attached to the underside of its belly. Raiza yelped in disgust, and kicked the wretched thing so hard that it flew through the air and landed with a splat in the darker waters.

"Finally, that delusional necromancer has left us alone…" The voice resonated throughout Raiza's skull. He gasped. The presence of a voice in his mind never ceased to terrify him, especially when he had thought it was gone.

"I never left you, Raiza. I simply stayed quiet whilst that idiotic excuse for a mage blabbed to you about necromancy and whatever else he thought you should know. I can't say that your new skill won't prove useful in the future, though. It's always good to have a few extra warriors to back you up, even if they are the living dead."

"Why do you keep talking to me? What do you want?" Raiza asked aloud.

"I want you to become strong. *I want you to be stronger than any other creature in all reality. I want you to* rule."

"Why me?"

"Because you are one of the most powerful beings in all of creation. I can help you use that power. I can unleash your true potential. All you must do is open your mind to me. All you have to do is let me in…"

Ultimate power sounded good to Raiza. "So, what do I have to do?"

"Yes, it does sound good, doesn't it." Raiza gasped. Could this entity read his thoughts?

"Yes, of course I can read your thoughts! I am a part of you. Now, relax, and open your mind. Think about nothing. That's it. Perfect. Now, I'm... coming... in!"

Raiza screamed. Suddenly, he felt a wave of confusion come over him, and his entire body seemed to tingle with some alien energy. He couldn't feel anything. He couldn't breathe! It was as if he was being dragged down into some dark pit of despair. Then, it all vanished. He felt strong. Stronger than he had ever been before. He roared an unearthly scream of elation as his body lifted into the air. He soared over the marshlands as bolts of energy leapt from his fingertips, before crashing into the earth below and detonating with ground-shaking force. He grinned at the destruction he had created. He felt *good.*

Now you and I are one, he found himself thinking. *I can control just as much of your body as you can. If you disagree with my actions, always remember that I have your best interests in mind.*

What do you mean? He thought back.

For example, if you wished to raise your hand, you could. If I wished for you to walk forward, that would happen too. But, if you tried to raise your hand, and I tried to lower it, it would result in a battle of wits between us. The winner's thoughts would take dominance. But let's not let that happen, shall we?

Raiza felt uneasy about that.

Don't feel uneasy. In exchange for partial control of your body, I have granted you more power than you have ever imagined before. With my aid, you can rule not just this universe, but yours as well. Together, we can be invincible. Look, see that hut below us?

Raiza glanced down. There was indeed a small wooden shack below, positioned on a rocky island sticking out of the swamp.

That is the hut belonging to the mage Valcoz sent you to kill. We wouldn't want to disappoint the old relic now, would we? Point at the hut!

Raiza pointed at it, and a beam of black energy lanced down to it, accompanied by a wave of ecstasy. Raiza couldn't help but laugh with pleasure as the hut exploded, sending wooden and straw shrapnel flying out over the swamp. Wood and straw, but no flesh; the Turbulent hadn't been in the shack. He was still alive.

It doesn't matter. We won't be returning to Valcoz. I've set my sights on a higher goal. But we can't become ruler of Mythicia until one little problem has been removed, the voice whispered.

What's that? Raiza asked.

Malcaractimus, the demon emperor.

"All aboard!" shouted Nick. "Medusa worms can't survive in water – if we can get this thing afloat, we'll be free as birds!"

"Units 1, 2 and 3, man the stern! Get pushing!" Silvanus immediately took command, and started firing orders at his elves as if he'd been on boats all his life. "The rest of you, man the rigging, hoist the sails, splice the splicy thing and all that palaver!"

The worms writhed and arched, streaming through the sand towards them. Silvanus' elves leapt from the deck, and began pushing on the stern, digging their heels into the sand and heaving their muscle-bound arms forward. But all the while, the worms were streaking closer, and closer.

The ship lurched forward, but so did the worms. They attacked the crew with incredibly ferocity, slashing at the elves with their deadly teeth. The ship moved again, and started to float. An eerie wind caught the sails, and –

“She’s sailing!” someone shouted. And indeed she was, and the pushing crew started to clamber aboard. Too late. The worms were upon them. Thomas could only look on in horror as two elves met the most terrible of fates, and were instantly consumed by the hideous creatures. The worms devoured their prey so quickly, the elves hardly had time to scream. But what little was left of the crew was safely on board and sailing away, leaving the raging worms increasingly far behind them as they escaped to sea.

Malcaractimus smiled menacingly down at Valcoz. The expression would seem almost friendly on any other face, but here it inspired only terror. “And so, necromancer, I am given to understand that you let the Fall escape.”

Valcoz trembled in fear. Every slave, soldier and mercenary under the demon emperor’s rule knew exactly how ferocious their master could be. If anyone failed him, he got angry. And when Malcaractimus got angry, people died.

“Master,” he whimpered, “The boy trusted me! He wanted to learn! I never even dreamed of him wanting to escape!”

“And yet he did, didn’t he...” The smile grew longer and wider, the demon emperor’s voice dripping with malice.

“It’s not my fault, lord, I-”

“Why did you let him out of your sight?” roared Malcaractimus. The smile vanished, engulfed in an eruption of rage.

“I’m sorry lord,” Valcoz whimpered. “I’ll find him! I’ll bring him back...”

Malcaractimus struck him to the floor with a strike that ripped the air from Valcoz’ lungs. He raised a hand to his cheek, and winced as it came away sticky with blood.

“You will not bring him back!” The demon roared even louder this time. “You’d just fail me again! No...” his voice dropped to an even more terrifying whisper. “I will summon Scorl. He shall not fail me as you did. The time of the prophecy approaches, Valcoz. Prometheus is gathering his forces. Soon, they will attempt an uprising against us! Without the child, we cannot succeed. Both the Destined and the Fall must both enter the circle on the night of the Black Star. Now, get out of my sight!”

Valcoz practically sprinted from the room. Scorl? Malcaractimus must want the boy more than Valcoz had thought. But what could a demon emperor possibly gain from a human boy? And how had the boy escaped? He had monitored him the entire time. He had just disappeared. Almost as if he had become a different person...

Chapter 10

The Raging Depths

Silvanus had taken naturally to steering the boat. Nick was fishing off the side, and trying, somewhat unsuccessfully, to catch dinner. Thomas and Alex had been appointed as cabin boys, and the three surviving elves were dotted around the ship, seeing to various tasks. One was up in the crow's nest, another keeping the sails in order, and the third was busy below decks.

Thomas, who found himself unneeded after nightfall, climbed up from below decks, and stood behind Silvanus, who was staring straight ahead out to sea.

"You should get some sleep," murmured Silvanus, his gaze unwavering as he kept his unexplained watch.

"So should you. Why don't we just drop anchor for the night?"

"I could never rest while Malcaractimus' demonic fist still clutches this universe," he said softly, firmly.

"Your staying up all night isn't going to stop him."

"I *have* to stop him. He kills everything that won't bow to him. Dryads, centaurs... my family."

"What?" asked Thomas.

"He killed them! My mother, father... even my little sisters! When he came to our home, we were told we either had to swear allegiance to the demons and become slaves... or die. My parents laid down their lives so that my sisters and I could escape. The demons chased us... and tore my sisters apart!"

He brushed his eye with the back of his hand, and Thomas realized that the normally strong elf was crying.

"That's why I have to stop him, Thomas," Silvanus continued. "He killed my family, so I have to kill him."

"I'm sorry," replied Thomas. He really was. The elf had been through an incredible ordeal. "I didn't know."

"Of course you didn't," Silvanus muttered bitterly. "You're just a kid. Everyone says you're the "Destined," the one prophesised to save all of us, and I don't doubt it. But how? How are you going to succeed where armies failed? Can you wipe out the demons? Can you free us all? Can you *bring my sisters back*?"

The words sent Thomas reeling. But Silvanus was right, how could he kill Malcaractimus? He was just a boy, so what if he could do a bit of magic? He was mixed up in something way over his head, and there was nothing he could do about it.

"You're right," Thomas murmured. "I can't. I just-"

"I know. Now leave me be."

Thomas nodded, aware that the elf needed to be alone, and hurried away. The silvery moon glittered down like a great eye, floating alone in the sky and fixing all with its ever-seeing glare. He settled at the bow of the boat, dangling his legs over the side as he watched the moon. *But not my moon,* he thought. Though it looked the same, he knew that silver disc in the sky wasn't the one he'd grown up looking at; that was a long, long way away. He wondered if he'd ever make it back there. In this universe, so full of threat, where peril was always just around the corner, it seemed plausible that he would probably die here. The thought of never seeing his family again caused a lump in his throat.

But why hadn't he died already? He'd survived so far on what could only be described as tremendous luck. Silvanus had arrived in the nick of time to save them from the archfiend, and as for the boat, what were the chances? A fully working ship left just lying on a beach? Something didn't quite add up, and whilst he wasn't going to complain about his fortune, he couldn't help wondering.

Shaking off his speculation, Thomas pulled his legs up, turned, and reached down to grab hold of an iron ring in the wooden floor. He pulled it upwards, lifting open the trap door that led to the cabins. It hadn't taken them long to find the various entrances after they'd set sail, and each was visible only through its ring. The panels had been made to blend invisibly into the deck of the ship – a defence system against pirates, Silvanus had speculated.

As Thomas swung down, closing the trap door behind him, the sea breeze disappeared, replaced by the musty smell of a long disused cabin. There were sleeping quarters for every man on the ship, joined by a long rectangular living room, into which Thomas had originally dropped. He walked roughly halfway down the cabin, and knocked on the third door on the right. There was the sound of a stirring and something clicking shut behind the door, and then it swung open, revealing Nick's kindly face.

"Ah, Thomas. Is it time for our lesson already? Do come on in." Nick stepped back, ushering Thomas inside. Nick's room was larger than Thomas', containing a single bed and a desk covered with charts. Nick followed Thomas' eye, and grinned. "Sea charts," he explained. "Found them under the bed. They're pretty old, but still readable." Nick led Thomas over to the desk, and gestured animatedly at the old, dishevelled papers. "This is where we're going, and where we were planning to land the *Beetle*," he said, pointing at a funny sort of circle in the middle of what was marked as the ocean. Pointing to it with a little black arrow was a half-worn away label. Thomas could make out an "A", an "L" and an "S", but the rest was just smudged markings.

"Amazing," Thomas remarked half-heartedly.

"Quite," the mage replied. Then he fixed Thomas with a piercing look. "Something's bothering you, what is it?"

"It's nothing," Thomas said, shaking his head. But Silvanus' words had hit home.

"No it's not. Tell me."

"Silvanus doesn't think I can save you all. He doesn't think I have the power, and he's right, I'm just a guy, I can't save the world I can't-"

Nick put a finger to his lips. "Thomas," he said softly. "You can't doubt yourself now. This goes beyond what Silvanus thinks. The prophecy goes beyond all of us. All my life, ever since this suffering started, I have believed in you. Way before you were even born, that prophecy was written, and I have never doubted it. And where we're going, there is a whole city of people who all believe in you and who *need* you to believe in yourself too. Because to them, you're more than just a "guy." You're more than just the Destined, even. You are hope. Do you understand?"

Thomas nodded. And he sort of did. Part of him wanted to shout and cry and scream at the world, but another, bigger part of him understood Nick. These people believed in him, and because of that, he had a duty to do his best not to let them down. Even if he couldn't stop Malcaractimus, he had to *try*.

"Now," Nick said. "Let's get on with locking away your Bloodrage. Have a seat."

Thomas lowered himself carefully onto a splintering old armchair. It creaked ominously, and Thomas winced as something cracked. Nick murmured a few words in True Speak, and just behind him, a miniature tornado span up out of nowhere, no more than three feet high. The mage grinned, and lowered himself onto the top of the tornado, leaving him gently bobbing in the air. He laughed quietly.

"I didn't think that would work," he chuckled. "Would have been embarrassing if I'd gone straight through. It's actually surprisingly comfy." And then he was suddenly serious. "These lessons may not be particularly pleasant, Thomas," he said gently. "If at any point you feel you don't want to continue, just say the word and we can stop. Are you ready?"

Thomas nodded. "Then close your eyes. I want you to slow your breathing to a deep and gentle pace. I'm going to count down from ten, with each number I want to you to slow your breathing more. Ten,"

Thomas took a deep breath, and let it out slowly. He took another breath, timing them with Nick's count. By the time the mage reached zero, Thomas was taking only five breaths every minute. He felt himself start to drift off to sleep.

Nick spoke again, softly. "Now I want you to reach out with your mind, and search for your power."

"Reach out with my mind?" Thomas breathed.

"Yes. Push out with your thoughts and find the source of your magic."

Nick still hadn't explained precisely how he was supposed to reach out with his mind, but he tried anyway. And then he felt it, a sort of lingering presence at the edge of his thoughts. He latched his thoughts onto it, and pushed at it with his own mind. He was surprised to find it pushed back.

"You can feel it, yes?"

Thomas nodded.

"Now don't try to overpower it, but visualise it." Nick leaned forward, and placed a hand on Thomas' forehead. "Siltheon."

The word echoed through Thomas' mind, and then he could see it, as though through a third eye. A pulsing, twisting orb of colour, sharper and brighter than anything else he'd ever seen.

"Now I want you to visualise a wall around it, and in that wall I want you to imagine a door."

Thomas did so, and in that third eye a red brick barrier formed around the sphere, and a few seconds later, a brown wooden door shimmered into view.

"And now, Thomas, I want you to open that door, and step inside."

Thomas willed the door open, and moved his consciousness through it and into the room he had constructed, the glowing orb suspended just as before. Thomas willed his consciousness towards it, and extended a metaphorical hand, brushing his fingers against the pulsing surface.

A mighty streak of pain forked through his mind, silencing all thought, leaving only nothingness behind. The "third eye" filled with white light, and Thomas gasped, his eyes flicking open. He was dimly aware of someone screaming, and only after a few seconds did he realise it was him.

He was lying on the floor. He knew this not only by the feel of the solid yet splintering wood beneath his back, but also by the aching pain in his head. He must have struck it when he fell. He felt an arm on his shoulder, and looked up to see Nick's concerned face peering down at him.

"I think," he said slowly, "that maybe we should give it a rest for now."

"But what happened?" Thomas asked, through shaky breaths.

"I have absolutely no idea," Nick replied, "But I don't think we should try to do it again. See you in the morning, Thomas."

Thomas allowed the gentle rolling of the ship over waves to rock him to sleep. He began to dream.

He stood on a floating platform over a barren landscape. A man was standing next to him, saying things Thomas couldn't quite hear. He raised his arms, and three zombie-like creatures rose from the ground in front of him. He felt strangely pleased with himself, as if he had passed some sort of test.

Then, he was flying over a swamp, lightning crackling from his fingertips. There was a voice, whispering to Thomas, but no one had spoken.

"Malcaractimus is a fool. He kills everything on the planets he captures, and has done with them. He should control and use *the worlds he dominates. That way, he could gain* true *power. Power I intend to seize. Together, that power can be ours. Together... we can rule!"*

Thomas woke with a start. *Well as dreams go*, he thought, *that was pretty weird*. Before he could ponder it more, however, the ship shook, and Thomas was thrown out of his bed and across the cabin. His head struck the wooden walls, sending a constellation of stars dancing across his vision. Hauling himself up, Thomas staggered out of the room and up onto the deck.

Everyone else was already up and about, waving weapons and shouting frantically at each other as they scurried across the ship. Nick and Alex stood by the mast, eyes closed, murmuring True Speak. Everything else was normal, except for the enormous tentacle draped over the side, thrashing about like a fish out of water. It was lined with black, poison dripping suckers. One unfortunate elf was struck by its spasms, and was flung screaming over the railing into the raging waters. He didn't resurface.

Alex and Nick snapped their eyes open and with a cry sent a bolt of white lightening arcing over the boat, striking the tentacle with an ear-splitting *"thoom!"* The great tendril flipped up into the air and plunged back into the deep, sizzling and crackling and setting the waves steaming. As soon as it hit the water, another tentacle shot out of the sea, wrapping round the mast. It suddenly tightened, snapping the pole in two. The main sail was ripped right down the middle, the two halves fluttering away across the oceans, carried by the wind.

By now, Silvanus and the two surviving elves had recovered from the initial shock, and were firing rounds of plasma into the giant limb, which only succeeded in making it thrash around even more wildly. The second tentacle had finished with the mast, and was striking at the various structures on deck, destroying all it touched.

The tentacle flailed out towards Thomas, whistling over his hastily ducking head. He rolled to avoid the tendril as it twisted in the air and whipped down at him, so close that Thomas could feel the dull throb of heat pulsing from the limb.

Then, as if that wasn't enough, a third tentacle reared up out of the water and crashed full against the boat, smashing through and dividing it into two distinct pieces. *There goes my cabin*, thought Thomas. As the half of the deck he was standing on started to tip at an alarming angle, water began to flood in onto the boat.

"Abandon ship!" Silvanus yelled.

"Come on!" Nick materialised beside Thomas. He grabbed him roughly by the sleeve of his jumpsuit, and dragged him towards a rickety-looking life-raft. Nick took a flying leap onto the raft, pulling Thomas with him, but as they were falling through the air, a fourth tentacle shot out of the water, wrapped round his waist, and dragged

Thomas down into the raging depths of the sea.

Opal stared up at the ceiling of her bedroom. The whole family had helped to paint it, and together it had taken them three hours. By the end of it, each and every one of them was blue in all visible places, except for Thomas, who had managed to paint his invisible places too.

Thomas. Where was he? Why couldn't he come back? And why had he gone in the first place? She turned in her bed, and closed her eyes. As she started to dream, her mind fell into a void of whirling colours and lights, swirling around her. It was always the same. Every one of the twelve nights Thomas had been gone, she had dreamt the same dream. Never anything different.

And yet there was something strange about it. She seemed far more aware in these dreams. She was conscious, and in complete control. She could move and think as if she was awake; the only thing she couldn't do was speak.

There. The colours had shifted, just as they always did. They were draining away from the space around her, leaving only darkness in their wake. And then they were gathering at one spot, one point directly ahead of her. They were taking shape. As each band of colour met another, it merged into a singled sphere, which grew with each band. As more swirls of light struck the sphere, it began to change, to lengthen and stretch itself upwards. Now it resembled a great thick pillar, solid amongst the dancing chaos.

The colours stopped converging, and faded into darkness, leaving only the pillar, a beacon shining in the void. Opal willed herself towards it, and she drifted forward. As she approached, a dozen coloured strands lashed out from the pillar, twisting through the dark before freezing in mid-movement. Their positions resembled branches, and so the pillar of light...

Must be a tree, she thought.

"Opal."

A voice sounded from somewhere in the blackness, and Opal realised it must have been the tree. No, this was different. In all her dreams up till now, she had merely floated before the tree. observing it and then waking. Never before had it addressed her. She willed herself closer, close enough to touch it. She reached out, and laid a palm against its trunk.

"Opal," the voice said again. "Sister of the Destined..."

She opened her mouth to reply, but no sound came out. She frowned, wishing she could speak.

"You can reply," the tree whispered. "Your thoughts are open to me."

Can you hear me? She thought.

"I can," the voice replied.

Where is my brother?

The voice was silent for a moment. "Drowning," it said.

Opal gasped. *What? Where? How?*

"He drowns on another world, alone and afraid."

Oh, God, Opal whispered. *Can't you save him?*

"No. I saved him and his friends before, but my powers are weaker than ever. The process of creating an entire ship out of nothing has drained me. No, I cannot save him. But you can."

How? Oh please, I'm begging you, just tell me how.

"All you have to do is dream. Dream of him, and dream how he can be saved. Send a dream to protect him."

A dream? Opal thought, and remembered a dream she had once had. She had been deep under the sea, swimming through the ocean, and while she was there she had had the tail of a dolphin. She pictured the dream, and as she did so one of the branches of colour lashed out and paused on her forehead.

"An ideal dream. With it, your brother can be saved, but not for long. By the Fall's hand shall he be wounded, but by the Fall's mind shall he be saved."

I don't understand! Opal pleaded.

"Soon, the Calling will sound for you. Be ready."

The dream started to fade. *No!* Opal protested. *Wait!*

"Trust in fate, child. Trust in the Destined..."

Thomas tried to gasp for air, but was rewarded with a mouthful of sea water. He tried to break free, but whatever monstrosity of the deep had hold of him wasn't about to let go in a hurry. His lungs began to burn. His whole life started to flash before his eyes; *So that really does happen*, he thought. Almost as if to taunt him, faces from his past leered out of the murky depths. His mother, whispering softly to him. "Why did you leave us, Thomas?" she said, glaring at him with murky eyes. His father beside her: "We need you..." Opal, his sister, laughing. "It's just like you to give up when it gets tough."

Thomas opened his mouth to reply, to tell her he hadn't given up, but more water gushed in and down his throat, clogging his lungs and making him choke. Then another face leaned out from the sea, but this one was strange and unfamiliar. Not a figure from his past. Why was his oxygen-starved brain conjuring up this? But then, the face winked, and pursed its lips. Impossibly It began to blow an enormous bubble of air, which engulfed Thomas' head and shoulders. He gasped in surprise. *Gasped*. He could breathe!

His vision clearing, Thomas saw that the face was attached to shoulders and arms, then a torso. But then, in place of legs there was... a tail. One great limb ending in a fan shaped fin. The person (if you could call it that) produced a glowing blue sword, which it then stabbed into the thick skin of the tentacle coiled tight around Thomas' waist. The iron grip slackened with a spurt of blood, releasing Thomas, who then swam to the figure's side.

It beckoned him, and swam away into the distance, before turning and beckoning again. Even breathing through a bubble, Thomas was a strong swimmer, but still found it hard to keep up with the strange creature with the dolphin tail.

He followed the dolphin-person across the ocean floor, darting between rows of coral and stone. Tiny silver and gold fishes darted between the rocks, shrinking back from Thomas as he swam towards them. Slowly, materialising as if out of a dream, an impossible sight drifted into view.

It was incredible. A colossal half-sphere, embedded on the seafloor like a titanic snow globe. It was clear, just like the bubble, and what light streamed down from the surface above twisted and glittered on the globe like some godly kaleidoscope. Many tall buildings stood within, similar to the skyscrapers Thomas had seen on holiday to New York.

The mermaid, for Thomas had decided that was what the strange girl was, took him by the hand and swam with him into the side of the great sphere. They melted through, and the clear revealed itself to be a film of some kind. Once inside, the bubble around Thomas' head dissolved, and he inhaled a long, deep breath of fresh air. Somehow, he and the creature next to him were floating above the rock below, but even as he looked, he saw it was not the seafloor, but a road.

Hand in hand, they drifted down to the ground, and the mermaid's tail split into two legs, mostly covered by a long silver dress, the same colour as her tail had been. Now they were out of water, Thomas could get a better look at the girl. She had long, dark brown hair that tumbled down around her shoulders. Her skin was a pale bronze, except for two blue scaly patches just behind and under her ears, and her eyes were a deep blue-green, deeper even than the sea she lived in. She wore a light, white sleeved shirt, but she walked barefoot.

"Hey," she said, giving Thomas a fleeting smile.

"Thanks," he began, "you saved my life. Had you not turned up, that... *thing* would have crushed the life out of me."

"It's nothing," she said, and shrugged, before turning and starting to walk away.

"Wait!" he called after her, "What's your name, and where are we?"

She turned and smiled again. "My name is Eve. Welcome to the ancient city of Atlantis."

"Atlantis?" Thomas asked, not surprised – nothing could surprise him any more – but intruiged. "Wasn't that some legendary city that sank into the ocean?"

"Sank?" Eve replied. "No, stupid, it *appeared* on the seafloor several thousand years ago. Where have you been for the past millennium?"

"Um... Earth?"

"Earth?" she laughed. Then, she looked straight at him. "Mind you, your ears are fairly round, and you're not tall enough to be an elf. But not short enough to be a beardless dwarf. Do you mean to say you're human?"

"Yes, as a matter of fact, I do. What about you? Are you a mermaid?"

"Yep! Sorry, but it's quite hard to believe you're actually human. I mean, they don't exist. At least, that's what I've been told. That's what we're all told. Still, if you think you're human, who am I to tell you different?

Thomas was amazed. "You actually believe me?"

"Um... yes. You'd have no reason to lie to me, would you? Come on, I'll show you where I live!"

Eve grabbed Thomas' hand again (causing him to turn bright red from ear to ear) and led him along a wide road lined with more skyscrapers. There must have been hundreds of different types of creatures coming in and out of the sliding doors. There were elves, merpeople like Eve, small fat, bearded people whom Thomas assumed to be dwarves, and a whole lot of fantastic myths besides. One that really caught Thomas' eye was a tall muscular man-cow thing. Its whole body was covered in dark brown fur, and appeared vaguely human from its neck down. Its head, however, was that of a bull, two large and menacing horns rearing out of its temples.

Eve followed his gaze. "That's Ranor. He's an ambassador of the Bull-King," she whispered. "Don't wind him up."

Eve pulled Thomas into a larger, more prominent building, blue and gold rings rotating around its shining walls. They were met by a tall, commanding figure, whom, by the scales behind his ears, Thomas assumed to be a merman.

"Who's this?" asked the merman.

"Thomas," Thomas said, extending his arm to the merman, but Eve cut him off with a torrent of excited babble.

"He says he's a human. I saved him from a very hungry kraken. Let's just say it won't be up for food again in a hurry."

The merman's eyes widened. "Another kraken attack? This is worse than I thought. That's the fourth attack this week." He turned to Thomas. "So, you're a human, eh? Nick's tinkering finally paid off? How is the old beggar by the way? Still strong I hope?"

"You know Nick?" asked Thomas.

"Oh, yeah," replied the merman, "We've worked together on more than one occasion. My name's Ingar, by the way. Now come inside – there's someone who'd like to meet you."

Thomas followed Ingar deeper into the building, Eve trailing behind. They entered a sort of reception, where an elf woman was waiting behind a desk. She nodded at Ingar, smiled at Eve, but then turned her gaze on Thomas.

Ingar spoke for him. "Ingar Swiftswim plus two. Here to see His Grace. Open up, Angela."

The elf nodded again, and flipped a switch concealed under her desk. The wall beside the desk slid open, revealing a stairway leading upwards.

"He's expecting you," said Angela.

Ingar led Thomas and Eve up the stairs, which twisted and turned like a snake. At the top, they came to a large metal door. Ingar pressed a button on a pad beside the door. "Ingar Swiftswim to see His Grace," he stated. He punched a code into the pad, and the door opened silently.

They stepped through into the most grand and magnificent room Thomas had ever imagined. The walls were gold, a red carpet gracing the floor. A large throne stood at the far side of the room, jewelled with ruby and sapphire gems. Seated on the throne was a broad shouldered and heavily garmented human. Or at least, he looked human.

He was neither old, nor young. His hair was neither long nor short. And the look on his face was neither happy nor sad. Everything about him was balanced – no feature was prominent.

“Welcome, child.” The voice was deep, and powerful. Thomas noted that both Ingar and Eve had dropped to one knee. He followed suit.

“Behold Prometheus!” cried a dwarf who had appeared beside the throne, reading from a scroll almost as big as him. “Bow before him,” the dwarf continued, “Prometheus, king of the Rebels, Scourge of Demons, Defender of the Ashes, Thief of Fire, Champion of the-”

“Give it a rest, Heston,” muttered Prometheus. He seemed to raise himself, and began to speak.

“My name is Prometheus, and I rule these lands,” he began. “Well, seas, as it happens. Now, who are you, and how did you come to the city of Atlantis?”

“Well, sir,” Thomas began, “it’s a long story.”

“We have plenty of time. If you will, I’ll be glad to hear it.”

Thomas stepped forward, and began to tell his tale.

Chapter 11

Scorl

Raiza relaxed on his black throne. He liked his new power. It had taken a while, but, with the aid of the Voice, he had managed to summon his own small army of half-lifes, and before long had had them dragging themselves to and fro collecting material for his own castle. They had finished the throne room, where he was sitting, but had run into trouble making the rest of the fortress – on the island where he had positioned himself, there was a big shortage of materials. They had begun to travel further and further away, and now there were days between each minion's return. It didn't matter though. He had all the time he needed.

There was the sound of footsteps outside. One of his undead minions had returned. The door creaked open, and yet no one seemed to enter. Curious. In his mind, he could sense the Voice snapping alert. Even as it did so, a beam of black energy struck out from a spot in the air just inside the door. Raiza leapt to one side, and the seat of the throne he had been sitting on cracked apart, smoking and fizzing dangerously.

Raiza heard more footsteps and another beam lanced out at him. He dropped to the floor, the dark energy singeing the hair off the top of his head. An abandoned brick lying in the corner floated up into the air, and hurled itself at Raiza. He dodged it, muttering "Sufemeron cefor" as he dropped to the floor.

Three half-lifes rose from the ground, each armed with a shield and spear. Another brick rose into the air, Raiza raised his hand, and the half-lifes lunged at the brick. There was a yelp of pain, and the brick shattered. A half-life flew into the air, and slammed into one of its comrades, as they collapsed in a heap. Another black beam pierced the heart of the third half-life, and kept going. Raiza tried to leap out of the way, but it lanced through his arm, leaving a smoking hole in its wake.

Raiza screamed in pain, but even as he did so, the hole began to knit itself back together, new flesh growing across his broken skin. He gasped in surprise. Something, probably the Voice, was healing him. That explained how his hand had grown back after the Voice tricked him into cutting it off!

The fool's invisible. The Voice sounded in Raiza's head. *Clearly, he's been sent to kill us. Invisibility is a common spell in an assassin's arsenal - luckily, every spell has a counter-spell. Now if you'll excuse me, I'll just quickly save your life.*

Raiza felt his arm rise upwards towards where yet another brick was being raised into the air. "Dipselcinan!" he heard himself cry. The brick froze in the air as an odd blue glow materialized around it in a shimmering aura. The blue glow expanded, enveloping everything around the brick in the same sheen. There was a sudden flash of light, and a thin, bony, blue creature stood in front of him, the brick still in its quivering hand. Slowly, a look of surprised uncertainty spread across the demon's face.

It leapt at Raiza as if it had been fired like an arrow. "Raskting!" the voice inside his mind cried. An arc of blue lightning shot from his fingertips, piercing the demon in the chest. It fell to the ground, convulsing hideously.

"Taeringt!"

The blue demon rose into the air.

Raiza still had some reign over his body, but had established a sort of harmony between himself and the voice in his head. He felt as if he really did have complete control, and his actions became his own. But he *knew* so *much*. He held in his mind a mastery of countless spells and rituals, endless tactics and strategies, and even had hold of the history of the universe. He and the Voice were now *one*.

"What is your name?" he asked the demon, softly.

"Scorl," it croaked.

"Why are you here?"

"No reason," it tried.

"Wrong." Raiza closed his hand into a fist. The demon screamed in pain. *"Try again."*

"All right, please, have mercy!" it squealed, "Malcaractimus sent me! He told me to incapacitate you! Please! He made me!"

"What were you told to do after you had incapacitated me?"

"I was to take you to his fortress!"

"Why did he want me at his fortress?"

"I don't know!"

"Wrong again." Raiza squeezed his fist tighter. The demon writhed.

"Please! I don't know! Something to do with a prophecy! I don't know anymore! Now please, let me go…"

Raiza stroked his chin, as if deep in thought. "No," he whispered. "I don't think so."

"What?"

"You really think you can come and try to capture *me*, and then expect to be let go? *Don't make me laugh*."

Raiza closed his hand completely, and then let go. The demon's screams echoed across the desert for what seemed like eternity.

"An intriguing tale. One that opens a whole new world of mystery for us to discover." Prometheus leaned forward on his throne. "Imagine how advanced we could become if we lived in harmony on "Earth"... humans and myths, working together. Such a shame that we could never visit it. There is so much to be learned."

Thomas frowned. "Nick and Alex managed to bring me to Mythicia easily enough."

Prometheus raised an eyebrow. "Indeed? I shall have to find out exactly how they did so another time. Technically, it isn't possible. Anyway, it is time to discuss your fate."

The doors slid open, and another dwarf hurried in. "Your Grace, we've picked up an incoming signal from the eastern islands. It's Nicholas, my lord. He wishes to speak with you."

"Ah," said the king. "My dear Thomas, it seems your friends have made contact. Receive the transmission!"

A wide, flat screen was lowered down from the ceiling on nearly invisible cords. It flickered into life, revealing a full profile of Nick's craggy, bearded face.

My lord, I'm afraid I have some bad news." The voice echoed out of concealed speakers surrounding the room. Nick's eyes widened as he saw Thomas. "Thomas! Thank the stars; I thought we'd lost you. How do you like Atlantis?"

"It's amazing!" Thomas noticed a stern look from Prometheus. "Sorry for interrupting, my lord."

"You are forgiven, my child. High mage Nicholas, state your location!"

Nick gave a quick salute. "After the ship went down, I thought we were goners, my lord. The life raft didn't last a minute - luckily, Alex had a quick water-breathing spell at the ready. We've washed up on some rather curious islands. Alex and I are both here, but we can't find Lieutenant Silvanus or his elves anywhere. We thought we'd lost Thomas as well, but I see he's there with you. Some of the island's local occupants make a tasty snack, so we caught and cooked them, and one of them thought this transmitter was also a tasty snack. It actually broke Alex's tooth whilst he was tucking in to a nice roast manticore. We managed to get it going again. Anyway... I called you just to let you know that we're on our way over. I hear Atlantian shipbuilders are very good."

Nick ended the transmission. He turned to Alex, gazing across the tropical beach and over into the jungle in the distance. A large volcano disrupted the otherwise flawless skyline. "OK," he began. "We've got good news and bad news. The good news is they've got Thomas over there. The bad news is we can't get to him. He's two thousand feet underwater. Any ideas?"

Alex was silent for a moment, and then a glimmer of hope began to form in his eyes. He blinked.

"Yes, Alex?"

"Well, couldn't we use a monolith gate?"

Nick looked uncertain. "And what, may I ask, makes you think that there's going to be one on this island?"

"I've got a hunch."

"A *hunch*?" Nick exclaimed, turning and striding away across the beach. "You want us to search an entire island full of less than friendly manticores, just because you have a *hunch* that there's a monolith gate here?"

"Unless you've got a better idea," Alex said, running to keep up with him, "then yes."

Nick rolled his eyes, "Well that's just *dandy* isn't it?"

Ten minutes later, the odd little pair reached the border of the tropical rainforest that hugged the foot of the mountain and sprawled across the island like a great green tumour. The undergrowth rose up to meet them, forming a wall between the blazing light of the beach and the thick, choking darkness of the jungle. Without wasting any time, Alex produced his trademark knife, and began slashing a path for them through the vines. Other than the sweltering heat, the repulsive smell and the incessant screeching coming from the trees, it looked like it would be a walk in the park.

"It might be helpful to know what we're looking for," Alex mused as he worked. "I mean, do all monolith gates look like stone circles?"

"All the ones I've ever seen do, yes. It's something to do with the arrangement of the stones over a certain magical fault line, but even I'm not too sure of how they work."

Alex nodded. He himself could count on one hand the number of times he'd used them. According to Nick, they were generally used for interplanetary travel by magi, and the best part was, demons couldn't use them. Nick believed that they probably knew about them, but simply didn't have the capacity to make them work. This gave the resistance a massive advantage over the Empire, but their far inferior numbers meant that even with the gates they couldn't achieve victory. They'd proved to be of even greater use, however, when he and Nick discovered a way to use the gate in a different way, to take them to an entirely separate universe, where in an unbelievable fluke they had found the Destined.

Alex suddenly had a thought. "Master?" he said.

"Yes, Alex?"

"When we were on Earth, we visited a similar thing to a monolith gate. I think it was called... Stonebend?"

"Stonehenge," Nick corrected him. "Yes, it's funny that Stonehenge should look so like a monolith gate. Perhaps Thomas can help us find the answer. But yes, we're looking for a circle of stones exactly like Stonehenge."

They continued to walk in silence.

"Master?" Alex said again.

"Yes?"

"I think I read somewhere there's some sort of theory that monolith gates can cause build-ups of pressure in the ground beneath. Something like that could cause a volcano, couldn't it? D'you still think there isn't going to be one?"

"Yep," replied Nick. "But it's our only hope. You're right about the volcano thing, but that doesn't mean all volcanoes have a monolith gate on top. Still, it's worth a try."

They carried on in silence. Moving through the dense undergrowth was gruelling work, and though Alex had his knife, he was having a hard time hacking through the ever-thickening plant-life that blocked their path. After several hours of sweating and aching beneath the glare of the sun, Alex gave a cry.

"We've hit rock, master!"

They had reached the foot of the volcano. Now they were closer, they could get a proper look at the sheer scale of the mountain they had to climb. It seemed impossible.

But necessary.

Chapter 12

The Island of Trolls

Thomas fell out of his bunk. *Again.* He had been given a room in an incredible towering hotel just off the side of Prometheus's building for the night. It was called the Pearl, and Thomas reckoned that if it was on Earth, seven stars wouldn't do it justice. The sheer size and magnificence of it was incomprehensible. Take his room, for instance. His bed had four different settings – Default, Water, Massage, and some bizzare option called Quick which he couldn't make head nor tale of. Ingar had returned to his family home, but Eve had been given a room next door to Thomas'. Apparently, her parents had died when she was young, and the hotel was her home until she was old enough to get a job. Thomas felt sorry for her, and was jolted by a pang of guilt as he remembered how he had left Earth without even thinking of his own mother and father. He missed them.

There was polite knock at the door.

"Come in," called Thomas.

Eve pushed the door open a crack. "Ingar's downstairs. We're to join him for breakfast in the lobby."

Thomas still found it hard to accept how this seemingly normal (and quite pretty) young girl was actually a mermaid. He grunted in response, and the door closed. Thomas quickly got dressed, and bolted out the door.

Breakfast... he thought. *Sounds good.*

He whizzed down the glittering spiral staircase that some magic made seem short despite the great height of the building, and skidded to a halt in the lobby. Ingar was waiting at a table with Eve, who was wearing a light blue dress, little pearl sequins sparkling in the light. Thomas pulled up a chair, and sat down heavily.

"Hi," said Eve, sheepishly. Ingar shot her a look, and she blushed.

"Glad you could join us, Thomas," he began. "We have much to discuss."

"Such as?" asked Thomas

"Such as the impending destruction of this city."

"Ah."

"Yes. We'll start with the kraken attacks. They've more than doubled in frequency over the past week. After your attack, I decide to take action, and swam out to the nearest kraken nest during the night." He pulled out a flashing red pad. It was small and square, and its pulse seemed somehow ominous. "I found this stuck to its inhabitant."

"What is it?" asked Thomas.

"We don't know. But whatever it is, it isn't natural. Someone, or some*thing*, put it there."

"Who?"

Ingar sighed, "I just said! We don't know! If we did, I would have told you, instead of saying, *"Someone, or some*thing*,"*."

"Sorry, sorry."

"Anyway, as I was saying, I want *you* to help *me* to get these objects away from the kraken colony nearest to our city. The one I ripped it off seemed to calm down when it was gone."

Thomas' jaw dropped open. "Hang on, hang on. You want *me* to swim down to the bottom of the sea, find a kraken, which, may I add, was exactly the same type of creature that nearly killed me last night, search it, steal a pad we're not even sure will *be* there, and get away without waking it up?"

"Well, you won't be alone, obviously."

"What?"

"*I'm* coming with you," said Eve, happily.

Thomas considered what he would have to face. He would have to swim deep down. Ingar and Eve could probably deal with that problem. He would have to sneak into a kraken's nest. His best bet would be to move quietly and strike while it slept. He would then have to take the pad off the kraken's body, which would probably wake it up. He hadn't the faintest notion of how to fight a kraken. But then with Eve...

"I'll do it."

The heat was rising, there was no denying it. Soon it would be almost too hot to keep walking. The higher Nick and Alex climbed up the mountain, the more infernal the temperature would become. Nick knew that unless the monolith gate was anywhere nearby, they would have to turn back and search elsewhere.

Suddenly, a stifled scream caught his attention. Nick turned to see Alex standing on a ledge, absolutely still, his eyes full of fear.

"There's something... on my... leg," he whispered.

Nick's eyes dropped. In the distance, he could hear manticores calling to each other with their strange wailing cries. But all that was blotted out by the bizarre image that now confronted him. A gnarled stone hand gripped Alex's ankle, stopping him from continuing up the slope. Then, slowly, the hand began to pull him to the floor.

Nick leapt towards him, at the same time pulling his staff out from under his shirt. He hit an invisible switch on its side, and the short stick extended into its full length with a click. He blasted a thin beam of light at the hand, shattering into hundreds of pieces. Instantly, another hand shot out of the earth and gripped Nick's wrist so hard, his staff slipped from his fingers and clattered to the ground.

Nick gasped, and used his remaining hand to fire small bolts of electricity randomly at the floor. Another arm rose, and grabbed Alex's leg before he could move. Two more shot up and tightened around Alex's neck, and dragged him to the floor.

Nick twisted his arm out of the stone creature's grip, and darted forward to Alex, desperately trying to pull the blond boy back to his feet, but the hands' grips only tightened. Slowly, ever so slowly, Alex's body began to meld into the earth.

He screamed as his arm was sucked into the soil, then his feet. Nick grabbed hold of the remaining arm, and pulled with all his strength, but nothing could halt his descent. The arm Nick was gripping slowly sank through the dust, leaving the mage clutching at soil. All Alex's half engulfed head had time to whisper before it too was pulled into the ground were the words:

"Remember me..."

It was perfect. Everything was perfect. Raiza smiled to himself, satisfied, and crushed his half-life minions into oblivion.

His palace was complete. There had been obstacles, of course. His half-lifes had finished the main structure of the buildings, but had been unable to add the details - chandeliers, paintings, and the rest. So, with the voice's knowledge, he had used his minions to craft these extras. Who would have thought that bones made such good building materials? Or that flesh could be woven and coloured to create such intricate paintings?

He sat, of course in his throne room, on his black chair of power. On either side of him stood a somewhat more powerful half-life. Each was dressed in black and red armour, and wielding a long and cruelly pointed spear. *Now*, he thought. Or was it the Voice? He couldn't tell anymore. *Time to make contact with the "emperor"*.

"Idnow Malcaractimus!" Raiza whispered.

The room was filled with an unearthly red glow, and a dull throb resonated from all directions. Then, a patch of crimson light materialized in front of him. It spread into a large, door-sized disc. Light and dark streaks of colour whirled inside the disk in a maelstrom of shades, blurring and twisting in all directions.

"Who dares wake me from my slumber?"

A demonic visage began to fill the disc, and roared the question like a lion. The head's long, curling horns quivered as he spoke, and the fiery eyes blazed brighter with every word.

"Do you not remember, me, Malcaractimus?" asked Raiza.

"Why would I possibly remember you, mortal?" the apparition boomed.

"Because I am not mortal, old friend. This human child is merely a vessel I shall possess until it is time for my metamorphosis."

"You?" The terrible face frowned. Then, it grinned, revealing two rows of sharpened, bloodstained teeth. "I'm glad you have returned, brother."

Nick sobbed into the earth, clutching desperately at the dust that Alex had once lain upon.

"No..." he whispered feebly, his normal aura of confidence evaporating by the second. "Not Alex," he moaned. "Not Alex. Not my son..."

It was something he had never told anyone. Not Thomas, not anyone he had ever met. Before the demon wars had reached his system, Nick had had a wife and family. Oh, it hurt to think back to the wars, but if he took his mind even further back, he could find bliss in his memories.

He had met Hope on the *Planet Hopper*, his first proper starship. He had been hired to transport materials from Frayme to Halora, in the Dewdrop system. There had been a crew of twelve on board the ship. Hope had been a secretary to the *Hopper*'s commanding officer, and during the journey, Nick and Hope had agreed to meet at a cantina for coffee. After that, everything had gone perfectly.

They had had a single child, whom they named Alexandros. And then, when Alex was six weeks old, the demons had begun their conquest of the galaxy, Nick had been called away into military service, and Hope had been killed.

Nick had returned to his home planet at the height of the war, where he had found Alexandros in an orphanage. He had taken him away, and had fled across the universe to Arcfied, where he lived for many years.

After losing the war, the Alliance had stopped on Arcfied to refuel, and had stumbled across Nick's home. They had been recruited as rebels, and the rest was history.

Alexandros had stayed with him for all this time, and Nick was glad of it. The name had been shortened to Alex, but the child was still Nick's. The only thing was, Alex had no idea that Nick was his father. He had been fifteen years old when Nick had collected him from the orphanage, and there had never seemed to be a right time to tell him. But Alex was all Nick had left of his past life. And *no one* was going to take his son away from him.

Alex couldn't see. He couldn't hear. He couldn't move. He couldn't do anything. It felt as if he had somehow been disconnected from his body – like he was a brain floating in a tank of water.

He wondered how he had got here, in this endless blackness. So dark. So cold. Who was he? He didn't know. His mind wasn't working properly. He needed to get back to Nick. Who was Nick? He didn't know. The lone thought seemed obscure, out of place in this endless black.

The name stuck in his mind. Nick. It was a point of safety, something familiar he could hold on to. He clutched at the thought, and tried to focus on it. He racked his mind, trying to penetrate the walls of fuzziness around the memory, but it was slipping away. No, he had to keep hold of it. He had to...

A speck of light appeared in the distance, faintly, almost non-existent. All thoughts of the name slipped away, and he shifted his focus to the light. It began to grow, wider and wider, bigger and bigger, and-

Pain shot through his mind. All the black went away, and consciousness came flooding back in agonizing waves. He could hear and see again. His wrists and ankles were burning, and he looked down to see he was tied to a slab of stone sticking out of the ground. His hands and feet were securely bound, and his head was ringing like mad.

Looking around through bleary eyes, he could see that the stone he was tied to was part of a circle. Beyond the circle, he could see all the island and the sea beyond, stretching out below him into the horizon.

I must be at the very top of the mountain, he thought. In the centre of the circle was a smoking crater, and hellish man-like creatures pranced around it, laughing and screeching.

"Wha happa...?" he murmured to himself.

He stared towards the hideous creatures, which had stopped prancing and started dropping pieces of rotten meat into the smoking hellhole. As each chunk of flesh fell through the gap, a bout of fire belched upwards with a cloud of black smoke.

Maybe they're cooking us dinner... Alex thought, hopefully.

Suddenly, one of the creatures spun round, and lumbered up to Alex. He guessed it was female, on account of its long hair, but he couldn't be sure, as various animal skins covered most of its body. Its face was hideous, warts rising like miniature hills off its yellowed, lumpy skin. Long tusks, like those of a walrus, grew from its mouth, and curled upwards towards the sky. When the creature spoke, they shot up and down like they were living creatures.

"Corzah?" the creature growled at him. "Thar'ohm? Lok mon Rok?"

I think it's trying to communicate, Alex thought.

"Español? Italiano? Deutsch? Français? New Elfish?"

"Yes!" cried Alex. "New Elfish!"

"New Elfish..." The creature laughed. It wasn't really a laugh. More of a throaty snigger.

"We trollsh," it growled, "I Kratchi."

Alex nodded. "Um... I human," he replied, mimicking the troll's speech. "I Alex. I friend. No nasty. Much happy. Untie ropes, please, and let Alex go? Muchly please?"

Kratchi sniggered again. "No! You not Alekz. You food! Food for the fire heart!"

Chapter 13

Father and Son

Nick extended his staff to a third of its full length, and moved it back and forth over the ground where Alex had disappeared. There was a faint bleep.

"Right..." Nick murmured to himself. He moved it along the stone a few inches to the right. There was another bleep. "Yes..." he murmured again. He moved the staff again, as if following an invisible trail. He was rewarded with yet another bleep, and then a ding.

"Aha!" he exclaimed, and excitedly ran along the cliff face.

"They took him down here..." he muttered. He clambered over a rock, and yet another bleep sounded.

He tripped on a pothole, and landed face first in a dry ditch. He stood up, dusted himself down, and waved his staff in the air, extending the pole it to its full length.

"Difn nsoym" he murmured.

Nick closed his eyes, opened them, and then opened them *again*.

The landscape around him was plastered with swirls of colour and light. Blue, misty streaks lined the sky, whilst crimson dagger lines sliced across the mountain-tops like thunderbolts. It was beautiful; every time he saw the world through magic took his breath away. But he hadn't found what he was looking for. *Wait!* Low along the path up to the cliff face hung a murky brown fog. He concentrated on it.

"No..." he whispered to himself. "It can't be..."

He had seen that fog before. It was troll residue. A unique magical signature, it only formed where trolls had used powerful magic. The brown fog started where Alex had disappeared, and stretched off along the cliffs. Amongst the dark pool of colours, however, there were odd flashes of silver, shining distantly out of the contrasting shadows. Now he was certain that it was trolls who had taken Alex.

Trolls were a tribal folk, and had a long way to go till they discovered space travel. There was an unwritten law in the galaxy that early-age planets were to be interfered with as little as possible, but even what little contact the trolls had had with the rest of the universe had been hostile to say the least. The monsters seemed "in tune" with the earth itself, and could draw magical energy from the ground beneath them, manipulating the Earth Discipline with incredible ease and ferocity.

Nick followed the brown until it trailed straight into the cliff-face, and so evidently the trolls had managed to continue straight through it. "Merctęas nom sęorin," he muttered. A white light surrounded Nick, engulfing him, growing brighter and brighter, hotter and hotter, before dropping the mage onto a dirty brown patch of rock. He was on the cliff side again. But this time, there were voices.

"You be quiet!" said the gravelly voice of a troll. "Stupid humans. Don't know about the fire heart! Don't know not to shout. Don't know when to keep quiet. Make big noise, fire heart spit flames."

"You wish! Maybe I will shut up, but only if you let me go! Nick will find me you know! He'll bring an army - plenty massive, much stabby, much killy!" The unmistakable tones of Alex rang across the mountainside, and Nick's heart skipped with hope. But this was only an illusion, a shadow of the past. What Nick was seeing now through magic had actually happened ten minutes ago.

A hideous procession marched across the stricken cliffs. The lead troll wore a silver crown, covering his long wispy hair. His tusks were studded with thorny spikes, but his face was decorated with countless warts and moles, each at least the size of a small pebble. He carried a mighty sword in his right claw, and an enormous banner in his left. The flag atop the banner was torn and bloodied, but an icon resembling a troll's hideous face, complete with tusks was clearly embroidered on the top.

Four smaller trolls followed the first, a large net slung between them. Inside the net, struggling furiously, was Alex.

Nick stepped towards the net. The trolls made no move to intercept him; in fact, they didn't even flinch. His hand passed straight through Alex as if they weren't there.

But of course, the troll's couldn't see or hear him. He wasn't technically there – it was like watching a film play out around him.

"Wait!" ordered the troll leader. He turned his head, and looked straight at the watcher. He started towards Nick.

He can't see me, he can't see me, Nick reassured himself.

He can't.

The troll lifted his sword.

He can't.

I think I'd better get out of the way.

The sword swung down, passing through Nick's head even as he tried to dart out of the way. He felt nothing. It hadn't touched him.

The sword had buried itself in a rock just behind them. There was a deep rumble, and the side of the rock barrier the group had come across began to slide out of the way with the faint whirring sound of hidden machinery. The procession began to move into the cavern, and the waiting onlooker was engulfed by white light.

Now Nick knew where his son was. And he was angry.

Chapter 14

The Gate

"All clear. Entering kraken nest now."

Thomas grinned nervously at Eve through his diving mask, and swam into the widening gap. He slipped the safety-catch off his harpoon gun, and pointed it forward, acting much more confident than he felt. Eve ignited her energy blade.

"Good luck, Thomas." Ingar's voice reassuringly crackled through Thomas' earpiece.

"Thanks," he replied. "I'll need it."

No sooner had the words left his mouth, than a long, dark tentacle whipped across Thomas' back, knocking the air out his lungs. Eve darted forward and slapped the tentacle away with the flat of her blade. It recoiled sharply, and Thomas had time to shine his torch on the creature's face.

Two shining red eyes glared back at him, and a large, toothed beak opened and closed hungrily. But Thomas didn't see the glowing eyes or the cruel beak. He was staring at the flashing red pad, pulsing menacingly between the creature's eyes.

"Target acquired," he muttered. "Permission to shoot?"

"Permission granted. Remember, just obtain the target, and get out of there."

"Why do we have to use this weird code? Why can't we just say "Can I shoot it?" instead of "Permission to shoot?""

"Stop arguing and just do it, OK?"

"Sorry, sorry."

Thomas fired, just as two more tendrils shot and around his waist. He ignored their crushing grip, and focused on the task at hand.

There was a hiss, and the hook snagged on the glowing pad. A strange hissing roar emanated from the kraken's den, and two more tentacle shot out of the gloom, and wrapped around his waist, crushing the air from his lungs. He struggled fiercely, hit the withdrawal switch on his harpoon, and the hook returned with a crack, dragging the pad with it. The tentacles relaxed, and the kraken shrank back into the darkness.

"Objective complete. Returning to base."

Thomas sighed, and started back to the city.

"I *really* don't like the look of this..." Alex muttered to himself.

The sun had set, and the trolls were spinning faster than ever now. They were chanting something strange in a hideous, grating tongue. *"Malto krassi, nis mouter Lok'Thor. Nis mouter Con'Cra. Nis mouter Dal'Tin..."*

The chanting carried on, endlessly. Kratchi had returned to her fellow trolls, and had joined the dance. Thunder crashed violently, and the clouds above them swirled like a writhing, living mass. A figure began to ascend the steps leading to the stone circle. It was the troll leader who had led their capture earlier. He no longer held aloft the hideous banner he had previously carried. The great sword was sheathed by his waist, and his hands hung loosely at his sides.

"*Trok'har*, my warriors!" he roared. "Be the human ready?"

Kratchi left the whirling dance, and knelt before the larger troll. "*Trok'har*, great one. The preparations be complete, yet no Fire Heart be waked yet."

"Good. I be just in time. We find another creature on mountain. It elf."

Alex looked on in horror as two more trolls climbed the steps to join their leader. Between them, struggling furiously, was Silvanus.

"Hi," the elf murmured with a weak grin.

"Hi," Alex replied. "Sorry to see you here. How are you then?"

"I have to say I've been better."

"What are they waiting for?" Alex asked wryly as the trolls bound Silvanus to the stone next to him. "If they're going to eat us, they'd better hurry up with it, before I die of boredom."

"Personally, I disagree. I'm happy for them to take their time. You survived as well, I see. Where's Nick?"

"I don't know. The trolls only took me."

Silvanus smiled. "Then there's still hope for us yet. Still, if they're going to eat us, why are they going through all these rituals and dances?

"Maybe it's a party?" Alex replied.

"Or maybe not."

The troll leader was slowly beginning to advance towards him.

"You come here."

Alex glanced at the ropes restraining him. "That might be difficult."

"What you mean?"

"I'm... err... a bit tied up at the moment."

"What you mean?"

"Umm... You've tied us up."

"What?"

"Ropes," Alex said slowly and carefully. *"You* have tied *us* up with... *ropes."* He indicated franticly at the ropes securing him to the stone.

Understanding seemed to dawn on the troll leader.

"Ahh... you want untie?"

"Yes. Muchly please."

"No."

As soon as the troll spoke, a tremendous crash shook the platform, and one of the dancing trolls was flung into the leader's back. He spun round, hurling the troll into another stone in the circle.

"WHAT BE THAT?" screamed the leader.

"That be me," said a voice.

The leader was flung off his feet by a searing stream of fire, and he howled in agony.

With a cry of *"Hitomas!"* Nick leaped into the circle, his staff blazing with blue flame. He roared at the trolls with fury.

"How dare you take my apprentice from me!" he screamed.

The leader rose to his feet, but was soon knocked back down again by one of his subjects, glowing blue and streaking through the air. Nick grinned.

"Ibonlvio!" he roared, and the glowing troll exploded in a shower of flesh and gore.

The crown-bearing troll again pulled himself to his feet, unsheathing his sword. Before Nick could raise his staff, the brute was on him, blade flailing wildly, but with tremendous force. It seemed to take all the mage's skill to block the blows.

Suddenly, his staff was knocked out of his hand, and was rolling down the mountain side. The troll smiled, raised his sword, and brought it down on Nick's neck.

"Any luck?" Thomas asked Ingar.

The merman stared down through his white microscope at the red pad. He squinted, adjusted a dial, and sighed.

"No. You go get some food. I'll let you know if anything comes up."

Thomas strode away, feeling good about himself. The kraken problem had been solved, with all the pads gone, but Ingar was still trying to decipher their purpose. Still, food sounded like a half-decent idea. He hadn't eaten since breakfast.

He casually made his way down the standard rebel-metal corridor, passing multiple locked doors. A faint whirring sound penetrated his peace. He stopped: the sound was coming from one of the doors on his left. He frowned and pressed his ear against it. The whirring sound had grown louder, and was now accompanied by a pulsing throb. Then

Thomas did something he knew he would regret - he opened the door.

What he saw seemed so completely out of place in this futuristic environment, he had to pinch himself to check he wasn't dreaming. It was a circle of stones. Large, granite slabs, carefully positioned in a perfect circle. Every couple of seconds, a throb emanated from the centre of the circle. Thomas took a step forward. Suddenly, a crackling orb of red lightning materialized a few metres in front of him. It seemed to be calling him.

"It's a monolith gate," said Eve.

Thomas jumped, and turned around. "How long have you been standing there?"

"Since you've been here. I saw you come in."

Thomas reached his hand out to touch the orb of energy.

"Don't touch it," she called.

Thomas snatched his hand away. "Why?"

"If you do, it'll take you away to another planet."

"Ah."

"Magi use them to get around. Do you want to see what's on the other side?"

"Can we?" Thomas said eagerly.

Eve stepped forward. "Tinfar cos mnti" she whispered.

The crackling orb of energy expanded into a blazing sphere of fire. The sphere grew, elongated, and stretched into a portal, tall and wide enough for Thomas to walk through with ease.

Slowly, the red began to drain away, revealing a chaotic scene.

Hideously deformed creatures were writhing and screeching like banshees, waving long curved blades. A taller, more prominent creature was scrabbling on top of a much smaller, frailer figure whom was only just blocking the larger's sword strikes. A glimpse of the smaller person's head revealed him to be-

"Nick!" shouted Thomas. Eve looked at him questioningly. "It's Nick! My friend! It looks like he's in trouble! We have to save him." He glanced at Eve. "Can I just go straight through?" he asked her.

"Well, yes, but-" Thomas leapt through the portal.

When Thomas had travelled to Mythicia, he had experienced an odd feeling of uncertainty, as if his body couldn't decide what he was. Travelling through the monolith gate now, he felt the same. He whirled through a madness of colours and sounds, his thoughts distorting into half made silhouettes. Then, some unspoken words formed in his head, joining the chaotic dance.

The Fall and the Destined, a broken lord.

The Destined's blade, an Ancient's sword.

The Fall will be felled, the Tears will restore.

The End will draw near, as it happened before.

In the Black Star's Shadow, in the circle of stones,

The Fall and the Destined, before the Throne of Bones,

Can release the Old Darkness, and break the last seal,

And all of Creation before the Dragon shall kneel.

And then the world shattered around him, the words were forgotten, and the vision ended.

He landed on a mountain top, in a similar circle of stones. The troll leader had Nick pinned to the ground, sword pointed at his neck. Thomas rushed towards him, his ruby-encrusted blade suddenly in his hand and the Bloodrage boiling through his mind.

"Storghlar!" he roared, and the troll found himself twenty feet up in the air. Thomas flew to face the struggling monster.

"Never. Ever. Mess with. My. Friends!" he said, and ran the troll through the chest.

The troll exploded, causing scraps of flesh and gore to rain down on the watchers below. The other trolls cowered in fear. Thomas landed, untied Alex and Silvanus from their stones, and helped Nick to his feet. There were many smiles and greetings all around, but all this was ruined when a booming voice echoed across the mountain.

"Thomas Colfrey..." echoed the deafening noise, like the sound of coffins clanging shut deep under the earth. All else was silent. *"At last the Destined is found."*

The clouds parted, and a metal platform began to descend from above. It landed silently, and a figure stepped down onto the earth. It was the last person Thomas ever expected to see in this place.

"What's up, nerd?" sneered Raiza.

Chapter 15

Dead Troll Walking

Raiza had hardly changed since Thomas last saw him. He was still slim, average height and of a rat-like complexion. Only two things told of change: the first, a fine layer of black stubble had formed across his chin, and the second was his eyes.

There had been a time when Raiza's eyes held only loathing for Thomas. Now, there was something more. Ambition blazed in those bright green eyes, and it was not hatred that they held for Thomas, so much as… fascination. As though Thomas was a rare type of butterfly; one destined to spend the rest of its existence pinned up on a wall above a little silver plaque.

"Sufemeron cefor!" Raiza called in True Speak. Five zombie-like creatures pulled themselves up from the earth around the circle, each clad in combat jackets and armed with machine guns.

"Surrender or die," he commanded coldly.

"What did they do to you…?" whispered Nick.

"Silence, old man!" roared Raiza. *"But to answer your question, I have… assimilated this child. Until my metamorphosis, I will be using this pitiful mortal as a vessel. I'm here for the Destined. Just hand him over quietly, and no one need be harmed."*

Thomas spoke up. Even though Raiza had troubled him so much back on Earth, he still felt a desire to protect him now. "I won't pretend to know what's happened to you," he said, "but you have no idea what you're mixed up in. Just leave. Come with us, and we can help you…"

"He doesn't need 'help'!" Raiza snapped. *"And he knew exactly what*

he was getting in to. He willingly invited me in. Now, Malcaractimus wants to see you, but he didn't specify whether he wanted you alive or dead. You have five seconds to walk over here and step on the platform, or I shall order my half-lifes to kill you all. One. Two..."

Thomas glanced at Nick. Nick didn't meet his gaze.

"Three. Four..."

Thomas panicked. What could he do?

"Five. Such a pity. Kill them."

The half-lifes lifted their weapons, and a blast of water poured from the centre of the circle, engulfing all five of them. The water swirled and stretched, and formed itself into a crystal clear ball, the zombies trapped struggling inside. Eve swam to the front in her mermaid form, and pushed her head through the surface.

"You can't survive for one minute without me, can you, Thomas?"

"Who's this?" Nick asked.

"Oh, I'm Eve," she replied, flashing one of her stunning smiles. "And yes, before you ask, I'm a mermaid."

"It's a pleasure," Nick said, smiling back.

Laughter echoed down from above. *"Despite such a heroic rescue, I'm afraid you're all still going to die."*

"He really is grumpy, isn't he?" commented Eve.

"Yes. He is," agreed Thomas.

"Ignore me at your peril!" raged Raiza. *"Hitomas gigantes!"* Raiza raised a finger, pointing menacingly at Eve's sphere of water. A great stream of fire shot from the claw, streaking towards the mermaid with a malevolent speed that seemed to bend the laws of reality itself. She

dived under with a yelp, but the flames hit the sphere and the entire thing evaporated in a cloud of steam. Eve fell into the dust, and lay terrifyingly still.

But Raiza wasn't finished yet. *"Sufemeron cefor!"* he roared.

As the spell echoed across the mountain, the sky turned dark, and the wind became cold and chilling. At a snail's pace, the fallen pieces of flesh that were scattered across the mountain top began to move. As if they were alive, they began to crawl towards each other, beginning the knit together like some strange, macabre jigsaw puzzle. The great sword, half buried in the ground, shot up and into a newly formed hand. Slowly, the troll leader sat up. Then, it stood. A demonic fire burned in each eye, staring outwards with dark rage.

Its blazing eyes blinked twice, and the troll limped towards them. Thomas hurried over to Eve. He touched a hand against her face, and her large brown eyes flickered open, staring up at him confusedly. "Can you open that portal?" he asked softly.

"Yes," Eve replied, seeing the resurrected troll and leaping to her feet. "But it'll take me a minute to set the destination. Alex and Nick," she said. "I'll need your help."

"Get going then," Thomas said, gazing up at the approaching monster. "I'll deal with this."

Eve gave a little scream and ran across the peak, diving for cover behind a stone of the monolith gate, Alex and Nick just a few steps behind her. She clasped her hands together, and began to mutter quietly and continuously, bright blue lights shining from her eyes. Nick and Alex both laid their own hands on the stones, and they joined in the spell.

Meanwhile, the troll had reached Thomas. It lifted its sword, and swung it at his head with the power of a tumbling mountain. Thomas brought his own weapon up against the troll's, parrying it with an almighty crash. The sheer force of the blow sent a blast of pain down Thomas' arm, numbing the whole limb up to his shoulder. Amazingly, however, the sword remained steady in his hand. The troll's face remained still as stone, expressionless in its onslaught.

Thomas stabbed with his own sword, but the troll gave an almost nonchalant flick of his blade, blocking the attack. Thomas' sword bounced off the troll's weapon like he'd struck against a wall, and he staggered backwards. Raiza cackled from above, and Thomas was struck by a bizarre similarity between his current battle and his fight with Lump and Boil what seemed like a lifetime ago. The troll moved forwards, slashing again and again. "Hitomas!" Thomas yelled, ducking beneath the strikes, and his sword blazed with blue fire. He thrust it into the troll's unarmoured leg, and the half-life staggered. For a moment it looked as though the creature would fall, but then it only straightened again and lifted its weapon again for another assault. Could nothing stop this thing?

Thomas glanced back at Nick. "Any chance you could hurry it up a bit?" he called. "Not long now," Nick replied, slipping the words in amongst his spell. Thomas tried to lift his to parry, but was rewarded only with a soft crunch. His sword wouldn't move – it was stuck in the troll's leg.

The troll's great sword came slashing down, and Thomas screamed in pain as the blade sliced deep across his shoulder. He dropped his sword, simply unable to hold on any longer and it rolled away across the dust. The troll's sword glinted in the light of the sun, and then Thomas felt Nick's hands on his shoulders, dragging him out of harm's way and into the now open monolith gate. Raiza screamed with rage as Thomas entered the glow, and knew nothing more.

For once, Malcaractimus had fallen silent. He hadn't spoken in days. His entire mind was occupied by a new emotion, one he hadn't known since his birth. Fear. Terror gripped him like never before. He tried desperately to understand the reasoning behind these irrational thoughts. His brother had returned. He should be pleased. But somehow, for whatever reason, his subconscious had awakened an instinct that had lain dormant amongst his race for millennia. Not since the First Demons Wars had demonkind felt fear. It must be his brother. Nothing else fitted. His brother's power far exceeded his own.

But why would his own brother possibly have anything against him? Well, not exactly his brother, but his blood brother. They had made a blood pact, which certainly made them as close to brothers two creatures could be without actually being born from the same womb. They had fought side by side in the first Demon Wars. Oh, Malcaractimus had been alive at the very beginnings of the invasion, but it had taken him thousands of years to become the leader he was now. But at the end of the first war, the arch-magi had imprisoned his brother. Imprisoned *his brother* under some wretched hill. They had transferred all their energy into a single suit of armour, and their champion had rode against his sibling, and had sealed him away beneath the battleground for all eternity. And then, to secure him away for ever, they had opened a dimensional rift, and sent the hill flying out and away to another universe.

But now, something must have awakened him. Whatever it was must have been immensely powerful. And now they had come to an agreement, Malcaractimus and his brother. They had agreed to remove the Empire's biggest threat. The Destined, or as he was better known, Thomas Colfrey.

The demon lord's throne room shook, and a blood red portal appeared before him. It widened, and the object of his terror stepped through.

Malcaractimus buried the ancient thoughts in the deepest chasms of his mind. He couldn't show fear in front of his brother. Fear was a weakness, and weakness was intolerable.

"I assume you were successful, brother," he intoned.

Amazingly, his brother shook his head.

"This body is weak. Clumsy. I could not fully utilize my powers. Soon, it will collapse. And yet his thoughts fight mine. He does not know it, yet he suppresses me. He has moments of control. And he has been poorly trained. His necromancy is premature. I would imagine Valcoz intended to refine the boy's powers before releasing him. Perhaps I should have let him. It would have been useful. Still, time is short. Soon the Destined will discover his true potential. That cannot be allowed to happen."

"No," agreed the demon. "It cannot. What happened?"

"The Destined and his cohorts escaped. I summoned a greater half-life, but they fled back through the monolith gate and sealed it. I could not pursue them."

Raiza's body convulsed, as an unseen battle raged internally. Malcaractimus shifted in his throne, intrigued.

"See how he fights me. It is futile, yet annoying. Remember our bargain, brother. I need the child. With the Destined's body, we can achieve total rule. Lend me your forces. With Escalma's aid, I can end the struggle. The Night of the Black Star shall come, and both the Destined and the Fall must be there to greet it!"

Malcaractimus considered this. "Very well," he concluded. "It will be as you ask."

"I cannot sufficiently express my gratitude," rasped his brother. *"And when I return, the Destined shall be at my side."*

Chapter 15

Captured

Thomas woke with a start, beads of sweat dripping from his forehead. *Another one of those weird dreams,* he thought. The images were still fixed in his head, only just fading away. Why was Raiza in his dreams? They couldn't be normal - that was for sure. But he wouldn't tell anyone. Something inside him wouldn't let him. There was no point, he told himself, in bothering the others until he found out the cause of the dreams himself.

Tonight, he had relived the battle on the troll mountain. But this time, he saw it from above, looking on in glee as the undead troll hacked at the Destined with impossible fury. The Destined... that was how he saw himself in the dream. For some reason Raiza knew him as the Destined. But that was strange. Raiza always called him Thomas, or at least "nerd". Raiza had certainly changed.

He got up. That was odd. A couple of scales lay on his pillow. As he picked them up, they crumbled to dust in his hand. *Interesting*, he thought. He got dressed, gathered what little possessions into a bag, and wandered out of his room.

"Hey," said Eve, just coming out of hers.

"Hey," Thomas replied. "Um, I just wanted to say, about last week, er..."

"Yes?" replied Eve, smiling.

"...thanks. You saved my life. Again. Without you we would all have died."

Eve sighed. "Is that all?" she asked.

"Er... um..."

Eve walked right up to him, planted a kiss on his cheek, then turned and strode away. Thomas blushed furiously. Then he realized he was hungry, and wandered downstairs, all thoughts of the dream disappearing from his mind.

Nick was waiting for him in the breakfast room. "Ah, Thomas. I trust you have told no one?"

Thomas nodded.

"Good. Malcaractimus' spies are everywhere, and if he knew where we were going next, it would put the entire mission in jeopardy."

"Couldn't I at least have told Eve?" he asked.

"No. I'm sorry, Thomas, but anyone will talk if put through enough torture. Come, the others are waiting."

A week had passed since they had returned from the troll island. On the second day, Ingar had called everyone together for a secret meeting.

"Welcome, my friends," the merman had begun, once the audience was seated. "There has been a breakthrough regarding the red pads,"

A screen flickered into life behind him, displaying one of the strange devices.

"Once our guest, Thomas, had retrieved them all from the kraken nests, I spent hour after hour studying them. They were transmitting a subsonic pulse, out of range of human hearing, but painfully loud for a kraken. It must have made merry Hell with their brain patterns.

"These pulses must have been the reason behind the increase in kraken attacks over the past months. However, this technology is far beyond anything we rebels have hold of. It's clearly demon-tech.

Malcaractimus' agents must have positioned them there.

"On the plus side, however, I also detected an interstellar-range transmitter installed on the device. I traced the signal to Panoga, in the Alamnia 2 star system. The Warring Planet. To be precise, I tracked it to this object."

The screen behind him flicked to a display of a gold helmet, spinning gently.

Nick gasped, quietly. Thomas lent over to him. "What?" he whispered.

"That helmet," Nick replied. "It's..."

"What?"

But Nick had fallen silent.

"This helm was the core device to the red-pad network," Ingar continued. "If we can get it back here, I can neutralise the signal, and after an analysis, it could bring rebel technology several steps forward.

"Now, due to the immense bravery they have shown over the past weeks, it is only right that I nominate Nicholas, Alex, Thomas and Silvanus to the task."

At this point, Silvanus gave a small cough, and got to his feet.

"With all due respect," the elf began, "I am unable to fulfil your request."

Ingar stopped. "Why is that, Lieutenant Silvanus?"

"I am returning to the Elethrien-Nasithra, where my fellow elven comrades reside. I have lost my troops, and Elven law dictates that as a consequence, I am relieved of both my title and my command. I have been ordered by the Council to end my mission."

And so it was that Alex, Nick and Thomas had arranged the secret meeting and departure. Silvanus was due to leave later that day.

They walked down the corridor, and stopped in front of the doorway Thomas had discovered only a week before. Alex met them outside.

"Ready?" he said. Alex nodded. Thomas shook his head. "What's the problem?" asked Nick. And then Thomas said it. "I can't do this anymore, Nick."

"What do you mean?" the mage asked, concerned.

"I want to go home. I *miss* my home. It's alright for both of you, you don't have families, but I have a mum, a dad, a sister... and they'll miss me!" Alex and Nick took a step back, surprised at the sudden onslaught.

"When you took me here, I'd just travelled between *universes*! I was tired, confused, and you," Thomas pointed a finger at Nick, "you launched into this great long explanation about demons and magic and everything, and then you asked me to join you! Well, I could hardly say no, could I?"

Tears flowed freely down Thomas' face now, and he closed his eyes for a moment, trying to regain control.

"Oh gods, Thomas," Nick breathed. "I had no idea-"

"Of course you didn't" Thomas snapped, opening his eyes again. "Of course you had no clue how some of the stuff made me feel. I'm fourteen years old, and now I've fought and killed demons, trolls, God knows what else. And now we're off on another "adventure," and I haven't a clue where we're even going. I'm blindly following you, trusting you. And I've had enough!"

Thomas slumped against the wall, sliding down and collapsing on the floor. He bunched his knees up against his chest, and lay there in a shivering, weeping ball.

"Thomas," Nick said gently, laying a hand on his shoulder. "What do you want us to do?"

"Send me home. You took me here, you can send me back."

Alex and Nick looked at each other. They had known this day would come, sooner or later. It had only ever been a matter of time. Alex crouched down beside Nick.

"Thomas, I hate to tell you this, but we can't send you back."

"Can't or won't?"

"Can't."

Thomas looked up at the blonde boy. "But you brought me here-"

"We brought you here using a fragment of Imaginarium. It's a stupidly rare metal, to such a point that I believe we used one of the only fragments in the universe. And Imaginarium has a practically unique ability. *It has the power to cross between universes*. Are you listening to me, Thomas?"

Thomas nodded.

"Good. We had three fragments in total – one of them we used to travel to your universe the first time. The second fragment Alex used to come and get you. And then, when *you* left, we used the third. Thomas, there's no Imaginarium left – we *can't* take you back."

"So you've trapped me here!" Thomas shouted, standing suddenly. "You've trapped me here, against my will!" he kicked the wall in anger. A few seconds passed. "Well then," he said, turning with a humourless smile on his face. "I've got no choice but to come with you then, have I?"

Nick shook his head sadly. "I promise we'll help you find a way back one day. Until then, you'll have to come with us. Now, are you ready?"

Thomas wiped the tears from his eyes, and nodded. Together, they opened the door, and entered the gate room.

Eve was waiting, cross legged in front of the monolith gate.

"Eve-" began Nick.

"I'm coming with you," she said adamantly.

"You're not. What would Ingar say?"

"I don't care. I've hardly ever left Atlantis. I've never even seen the stars. Please, take me. I want to see the universe."

"Ingar will be worried."

"I left him a note. Face it, I'm coming whether you want me or not."

Thomas looked at Eve quizzically. "How did you know we were leaving?" he asked.

"Your bag. When I saw you just now, you'd filled your backpack. You'd left nothing in your room."

Nick sighed. "Thomas, why can't you be more careful?" he asked, exasperated.

Thomas looked at his feet.

"Well, we'd better get going then," muttered Nick

Eve's eyes filled with hope. "So you'll take me?" she asked.

"If we don't you'll just follow us." Nick turned to the circle of stones. *"Taeth yut so ditun korsant sidser, ido en Panoga,"* he cried. The familiar crackling orb appeared, and began to expand upwards and sideways.

An image began to appear in the portal. It was a dark forest; most of the sun's light being blotted out by a canopy of leaves. Nick stepped through, followed by Alex. Only Thomas and Eve were left now. He glanced at her, and she returned his gaze. In the flickering light of the monolith gate, she looked stunningly beautiful, and Thomas' heart raced his eyes met hers. Eve reached out and took his hand, her palm warm and soft against his. She smiled shyly, and together they stepped through the portal.

The forest looked exactly like it had through the portal – a sylvan glade of towering trees, each as tall as a small building, branches breaking away from the top, and fanning out into multiple spreads of leaves, blocking all light from the small clearing below.

The first thing Thomas was aware of, as he stepped out onto the rough carpet of roots and leaves, was the smell. A pure, overpowering scent that he could only describe as the smell of nature rushed into his nostrils, the moist air settling on his hands and face.

The group huddled together in the oddly-shaped shadows, whilst Nick began to outline the plan. First, they were to find a way out of the forest. Ingar had traced the helm to an underground fortress, situated just outside the woods. Once there, they would sneak in undetected, and find the transmitting helmet guarded in the treasure room.

"How are we going to get out?" asked Thomas.

Nick glanced down at Thomas' hand, noticing how tightly it was gripping Eve's. He quickly looked away. "Well," he began. "We'll run away, I suppose."

Eve looked sceptically at him.

"Very quickly?" he suggested feebly.

"You really haven't thought this through, have you?" she said, as if she were talking to a toddler.

How the mage reacted to this statement will never be known, as just as Nick was about to reply, an unearthly screech filled the forest. Hundreds of other voices took up the cry.

The four of them froze, and scanned the clearing, nervously. After several seconds, Thomas realized he had been holding his breath, and gasped for air. There was a sharp *thwack*, and a green-flecked spear embedded itself in the tree trunk beside him. He turned, pulled the still-quivering weapon out, and looked at it.

As he did so, a spider scuttled out of the trees. It was as big as a large dog, and on its back sat a little green man, no taller than a child. The man had a long, comical nose, a single red wart growing off the tip. Two large round ears stuck out of his head like dinner plates, and they quivered as he spoke. He was holding a short sword, and was grinning like a mad person.

"*Snelch gwilf werctar!*" it cried in a high pitched voice.

In response, several other green men scuttled into the clearing, blocking any possible escape. Each rode a large black spider, and every one of them was grinning inanely. Some held spears, similar to the one that had just missed Thomas.

"*Gwold niff swelchar?*" one of them asked Nick.

"Er... *wig swelchar Nick. Tis swelchar Alex, Thomas, allo Eve,*" he replied, indicating each of them in turn.

"What are they?" whispered Alex.

"Goblins," Nick whispered back. "They don't speak New Elfish. So we can talk freely."

"Fold wiff wiff?" demanded the goblin.

Nick returned to conversation with the snotty little creature. The thing's voice rose and rose in pitch as he spoke. As the conversation reached a screeching climax, the creature actually jumped with excitement. After several more minutes of nattering speech, Nick turned to them.

"Are they letting us go?" Thomas asked him.

"Err... that is... err... no."

"No?" Eve asked incredulously.

"No. They're quite proud of themselves for capturing us. So... they want to keep us."

"What for?"

"Pets. They want to keep us as pets."

Chapter 16

The Warring Planet

Thomas woke up, and *didn't* fall out of his bunk. If he could have done, he would have done, because that kind of narrative certainty is present in all universes. But he didn't, simply because he wasn't in a bunk. He was upside down. To be precise, he was in a net. Dangling, upside down in a net. It was hanging from the ceiling. He stared up at it through the darkness. It was hard to see, as there was precious little light, but he was fairly sure it was made of hard grey rock, naturally formed by the look of the stalactites that drooped mournfully down towards the floor. The walls were made of the same stone, as was the ground. He must be in some sort of cave.

Hanging from a similar net beside him was Alex. He was snoring loudly.

"Hey!" Thomas whispered across the cave.

"Sngrhnf…"

"Wake up!"

"Notnowmumimsleepin…"

"WAKE UP!"

Alex shot upright, knocked his head on the ceiling, and fell back down, dazed.

"Wha…" he murmered.

"Where are we?" Thomas whispered again.

Alex lifted his head and looked around.

"We're in a cave," he concluded.

"I can see *that*," Thomas snapped. "Where *are* we?"

"How am I supposed to know? They drugged me as well, you know."

Thomas grudgingly remembered what had happened the night before. No sooner had Nick explained the goblins' intentions than the little green creatures pounced, straight on to them. Thomas had fought, as had the others, but to no avail. They had been drugged, and carried back to wherever in Mythicia they were. As for Nick and Eve, who knew? Thomas had to assume they were being held in another cave.

He scrabbled around in the net for a few moments, and managed to right himself. As he struggled, a flash of orange caught his eye. A small, pointed head was poking out from a crack in the wall. It sniffed, and pulled itself out into the open. It looked like a normal, baby fox. It *acted* like a normal, baby fox. But it wasn't. It had nine tails. It wandered nonchalantly into the centre of the cave. Then, its tails started spinning like helicopter rotors, and it rose steadily into the air.

Thomas stared at it in amazement. It drifted upwards, and alighted on Thomas' right foot, which was sticking out through the netting. The tails stopped spinning. It nuzzled his shoe, and pushed itself inside. Thomas smiled at it, and laughed as it buried its head in his chest.

"He likes you," Alex commented.

Thomas stroked it, gently. The fox looked up at him. Its eyes were a bright, shining blue. It turned, and jumped back onto his foot. Thomas sighed, disappointedly. The fox growled quietly. Its tails began spinning again, but it didn't take off. It closed its eyes. Suddenly, flame shot from the fox's mouth, and the netting it struck burned away. There was now a gap just big enough for Thomas to fit his head through.

"Nice one, little buddy," he said, a grin spreading across his face.

The fox seemed pleased. It turned, and breathed again. More of the netting burned away.

"It might be good if you stopped now," Thomas said, the grin fading.

But the fox ignored him. The steady stream of flame flowed from its mouth, and soon the entire bottom of the net was gone. Thomas suddenly realized that there was nothing holding him up any more. He yelped, and plummeted downwards.

The fox's tails spun, and it grabbed hold of his arm. Impossibly, although it clearly took a lot of effort, the fox was holding him up in the air. It gently lowered him to the ground, and flew back up, towards Alex's net. It repeated the process, and soon Alex was standing beside him.

The fox ran up Thomas' leg, and sat on his shoulder. Thomas turned on the spot, and looked around the cave. "Alex," he said quietly.

"Yeah?" the boy replied.

"There's no exit."

And it was true. There wasn't a single gap in the wall, anywhere. No doors, no windows, nothing. They may have escaped the nets, but they were trapped in the cave itself.

"You're right," Alex said, his face grim.

"If only we had more light," Thomas muttered. "There must be a lever somewhere-"

"Stop!" Alex shouted so abruptly that Thomas jumped.

"What?" he asked.

"Say it again."

"What, "what"?"

"No, the bit about light."

"Oh. "If only we had more light?""

"But that's it! Light! There shouldn't be any. We're in a completely sealed off cave. It should be pitch black!"

Thomas frowned. "That's true..." he said. "So where's the light coming from?"

They were silent for a moment, scanning the walls for a break in the stone, but there was none. And then something occurred to Thomas.

"Where's the fox gone?" The creature had vanished. It was nowhere in the cave.

"Maybe it's gone back down its hole?" Alex volunteered.

"Maybe."

And then the fox trotted back into the room. Not up through the hole. No, it had actually walked straight in. Through the wall itself. It shook itself, puffed a ball of smoke from its nostrils. And walked back through. Thomas and Alex both stared at it.

"Of course!" Alex cried. He ran after the fox, and disappeared through the wall as well. Thomas was still staring. "What..." he murmured. And then he jumped to see Alex's arm emerge through the stone, grasping at the air. A part of his face came through as well.

"It's an illusion," the part of Alex's face explained. "That's why there was light! Because there's nothing to stop it coming through! The wall isn't actually there!" He grabbed hold of Thomas, and before he could protest, Alex pulled him through the wall as well. It was the queerest sensation, Thomas thought as he fell through the stone. He naturally expected a solid barrier to block him, but he just slid straight through.

He stumbled out the other side, and Alex grabbed him by the arm. A dim lamp hung from the ceiling, revealing the source of the mysterious light. Another tunnel stretched off into the distance. Together, Thomas Alex and the fox wandered into the tunnel, and away beneath the ground.

Soon, it became too dark to see. They started feeling their way. The fox dug its claws deeper into Thomas' shirt, and clutched him tightly, as a baby clutches its mother. Thomas felt it tense, and the fox began to glow, faintly at first, but the orange glow gradually grew brighter, and brighter, until they could see every detail in perfect clarity. They continued in silence.

Suddenly, they stopped. They had reached a fork in the tunnel. Three possible pathways presented themselves.

"We should choose carefully," advised Alex.

"One way's as good as any, surely," Thomas replied.

"No. There are bound to be traps."

Thomas hadn't thought of that. But Alex was correct. Of course there would be traps. But each tunnel looked exactly the same. There was no way of knowing which way was right.

The fox hopped down off Thomas' shoulder. It cautiously approached the left-hand tunnel, its tails twirling nonchalantly. It sniffed. Then it darted back to Thomas.

"Not that one then," he observed.

The fox padded over to the middle tunnel, and before they could stop it, it bounded off excitedly. Alex and Thomas blinked, and bounded after it.

The tunnel seemed to go on forever, yet the ever dwindling light of the nine-tailed fox remained distant. Finally, it stopped. When they caught up with it, they found themselves in a large cavern, similar to the one they had started in. Two nets were hanging from the ceiling. In one of them, struggling furiously was Eve. In the other was Nick. His eyes were closed, and his skin had taken on a worrying blue tinge.

Eve spotted them. "Oh, hello!" She called down. "Good morning. Or possibly evening. Perhaps lunchtime. There's no way of knowing."

"Are you alright?" Thomas called back.

"I'm fine, but I'm worried about Nick. He won't wake up!"

"Wait one second!"

Thomas gently lifted the fox off the ground. He pointed it towards the nets. The fox's tails whirred, and soon Eve and Nick were on the ground. Eve stood up. Thomas ran over to Nick.

"Come on, Nick," he muttered, kneeling over the old mage. "Wake up!"

No response.

"We'll have to carry him."

Alex looked thoughtful "We could, I suppose. But it would be hard, and we could hardly sneak out with him on our backs."

Thomas thought about this. "Anyone know a lifting spell?" they looked at each other, sheepishly. Suddenly, there was a commotion in the tunnel beyond.

"Quick!" said Alex. "We've got company!"

Thomas and Alex half dragged-half carried Nick behind a small pile of rocks. Eve hurried after them, and together they flattened against the ground. There was a small gap in the stones, and Thomas used it to look through into the main cavern.

A dozen goblins poured in, yelling and screeching like animals. The front goblin was wearing a robe, and was twirling a black sceptre in his hand. On his head, he wore a golden helmet, although it seemed a couple of sizes too big for him.

"Snelch wiff welch snergle-dergle?" he cried, pointing at the broken nets.

The other goblins shifted from foot to foot uneasily. Nick groaned quietly in his sleep. Thomas hastily covered his mouth with his hand.

"Why are the nets broken?" he murmured.

"Shut up!" hissed Thomas.

"Snilch welch niggle-piggle-diggle?"

"Who was responsible for guarding the nets?" Nick murmured again.

Realization dawned on Thomas. Some instinct inside the mage was still working, and he was subconsciously translating the goblin speech.

One of the goblins uneasily stepped forward. *"Sniggle-swelch swag scooplesneer…"* he said, quietly.

"It was my job…" translated Nick.

"Snaggle scooplesneer squog squog?" demanded the king goblin.

"And why were you not at your post?"

"Giggity swiggle Gorg swish fig-swig. Iggle quack! Snargle blom nom nood!"

"Gorg and I went for a drink. I'm sorry! They were unconscious!"

"Snarg…" murmured the king.

"Fool…"

"Iggle quack! Iggle quack! Ligs globby!"

"I'm sorry! I'm sorry! Have mercy!"

The king raised his sceptre menacingly, pointed it at the cowering goblin, and smiled.

The goblin screamed a long, high pitched scream, and began to burn. It was engulfed by green flames, growing brighter and brighter until Thomas had to look away. When the light died, all that was left was a pile of ashes. But then Nick began to scream as well. Long and plaintive, it was a perfect copy of the sound the late goblin had just made.

Immediately the king's head whipped round, focusing directly on the place where Thomas was hiding.

"Scwill dras cumec?"

"Who screamed?" Nick translated.

Slowly, the goblin advanced menacingly towards the pile of rocks.

"Gintor cwick nistor digts pur."

"Come out with your hands up."

"Twill crass dinst. Gintor cwick nistor digts pur, coum nis crisstor srag!"

"I will not tell you again. Come out with your hands up, or I will blow you to smithereens!"

Slowly, indicating the others to follow, Thomas raised his hands and stood up. Alex and Eve grabbed one of Nick's arms each, and dragged him out.

"Hmm..." the king smiled. "The escaped... prisoners."

"You speak New Elfish?" Thomas asked, surprised.

The goblin placed his thumb and forefingers close to each other.

"A little. How did you... get out of my... nets?"

Thomas glanced at the fox, who was still cowering behind the rocks.

"They, err, they broke!" he looked at the others meaningfully. *"Didn't they*?"

"Er... yes," agreed Alex. "They broke."

"Hm... I see," observed the goblin. "You will come with me. I have a... a..."

"A what?"

"A... bucket full of eels.

"What?" asked Thomas, bemused.

"Perhaps my New Elfish is not as good as I thought... never mind. You will observe!"

However, it was never discovered what the goblin truly meant, as at that point, the ground shook with such tremendous force that the corners of Thomas' vision greyed out.

"Sneelch weelch beelch neelch!" screeched the king.

The goblins leapt on to their separate spiders, and scurried off into the tunnels.

Thomas suddenly got the feeling he'd missed something important. "Hang on..." he said. "Why didn't Nick translate?"

"Because I'm awake," replied Nick. "But if you must know, it means "Siege engines!""

Nick was leaning groggily on Alex's shoulder. Some of the blue tinge had left his face, but it still lingered on the edges of his lips and at the sides of his eyelids.

"Are you all right?" Thomas asked.

"I'm fine," Nick replied. He took a step forward, and crumpled. Alex just managed to catch him before he hit the ground.

"No, you're not," Eve cautioned him. "You nearly died. Just take it easy, and let us help you."

Nick grudgingly lent on Alex again. "All right, matron, I'll take it easy. But my spells are still fine!"

"What happened back there?" asked Thomas. "Why did the ground shake like that?"

"The goblins aren't the only creatures on this planet," Nick explained. "They share it with another, considerably tougher race."

"Who?" asked Eve.

"Orcs. Big green skinned brutes who really work out. Fists the size of bowling balls. Not particularly bright, I think you'll find."

"Oh," said Thomas. "And they're here?"

"I think we're about to find out."

The ceiling broke. One moment there was rock above them, the next, rock was falling all around them. A rope unfurled through the hole and hung innocently in the centre of the cavern.

"Goargh Hargh!" came the cry from above. Thomas stepped back, and suddenly his jewel encrusted sword was in his hand. But he had lost it on the troll mountain. How could it be here now? Before he had time to think about it any further, three tall burly green men slid down the rope and stood, feet planted firmly on the ground, in front of them. They each wore plain black T-shirts, and strange leather shorts. Wordlessly, one of them stepped forward and picked Thomas up by the

legs, dangling him upside down.

"Gish noarg?" he asked.

Thomas smiled, nodded, drew his jewel-encrusted sword and stabbed the creature through the chest. The orc fell backwards, a look of surprise on his face. One of the other orcs fumbled in his pocket and produced a handgun. He fired at Thomas three times.

The first bullet whizzed past his head and embedded itself in the wall. Another hit the space between Thomas' feet. The third missed completely, ricocheted off a piece of jagged metal sticking out of the ground, and hit the other orc in the foot.

It crashed to the ground, but the first orc was just placing another magazine into his gun.

"Threa masch!" cried Nick, raising his staff. The ground beneath the remaining orc's feet split open, and the creature suddenly found itself buried up to its neck in solid rock. It gasped, its eyes rolled, and the head lay still.

The wounded orc was pulling itself to its feet again.

These things just don't give up, do they? Thomas thought.

It produced its own handgun, and pointed it at Nick.

"Hitomas!" shouted Thomas. His sword ignited, and he hurled it at the green brute. The sword impaled the thing in its muscle-bound chest, and the creature roared in pain. It was engulfed in a flickering blue flame, and when the light died, the orc had been reduced to a pile of ashes.

There were noises from above. More orcs began to descend the rope, snarling.

"Let's get out of here!" Eve shouted.

Thomas snatched up his sword, and they ran.

Chapter 17

"Orcses!"

The nine-tailed fox leading the way, they fled from tunnel to tunnel, never looking back. The narrow path opened up again, and they found themselves in another cavern. There was no exit. The only way back was the way they had come. Thomas began to double back, but the sound of tramping feet made him think again. Nick was muttering something under his breath.

"Tarng su vynsiibisitil ot dieh su mrof ergen-nisks," he began. "Kasm uor nseet mrof tiehr seons. Ctreopt su, o gimac."

Thomas glanced at him. Nick smiled, and raised a finger to his lips. As he did so, a squad of orcs jogged in, guns in hand. Thomas had quickly prepared a convincing beg for mercy, and dropped to his knees. But the orcs didn't acknowledge him. They walked straight past, and into the next tunnel.

"Invisibility spell," explained Nick. They can't see us, and they can't smell us. We can hide from anything orcish. But they *can* hear us, so keep quiet."

The distant tramping of orcish feet grew fainter, and soon was silent. They wondered down the passage after the orcs.

Alex's feet hurt. He was tired of walking. He wanted to – needed to rest. This was stupid. A quick spell, and they could be up and out the hole the orcs had come through in no time. But *no*, they had to go and find this "ever-so-special" helmet. And to top it off, his shoelace was undone. He bent to tie it, and was suddenly aware of an odd low hissing noise behind him, like a bleeding radiator. He turned, and screamed.

The noise turned to stone on his lips.

Commander Krak'Gragh was a simple creature. Or at least, simple in the way that orcs go. His life consisted of three main activities: Fighting, eating and sleeping. Currently, he was engaged in the former of the trio. He was, to be exact, underneath a large pile of screaming goblins, or as he liked to call them, snotties. He didn't have a particularly large vocabulary, but then again, his tennis-ball sized brain reasoned that vocabulary played no part in killing goblins, and thus was not needed.

He twitched, and a swathe of snotties tumbled off the writhing heap. Then he stood up, causing a miniature green volcanic eruption. He unsheathed his stick. He liked his stick. He especially liked the lump on the end of it. The spiky one. He'd once heard someone call his stick a club, but he dismissed it as idiocy – there was no way a party could be going on inside a stick. He grunted, and swung his stick.

His stick, he decided, was a magic stick. He believed this, because any snotties it hit at speed seemed to suddenly gain the ability to fly, and did so, clearly enjoying it by the high pitched laughter they loosed as they flew.

He smiled, and hit another snottie.

Thomas heard the sounds of the fight before they reached the cavern in which it was taking place.

"Sounds exciting," he muttered.

"It's the only way," Nick explained.

"How do *you* know?"

Nick tapped the side of his nose conspiratorially, "Secret."

"You've got a map, haven't you?"

"Yes," Nick admitted. He produced a soggy ball of crumpled paper from the folds of his robe. Once he had finally managed to unfurl the wretched thing, he squinted at the faded text drawn on it.

"I really, really need glasses," he muttered.

A goblin flew through the opening, and knocked Eve to the ground. She hastily brushed herself down, and backed away. The goblin shook itself, and drew its dagger.

"*Snelf wiff wiff?*" it asked hesitantly.

Nick smiled. "Btinid."

The creature suddenly found itself unable to move. The knife fell from its quivering hands.

"What's happening in there?" he whispered menacingly.

"Orcses!" the goblin squealed. "Orcses is killing us! Great big one, big stick! Knocks us goblinses down. But Swerg gets up again, Swerg finds pink-skins! Swerg kill pink-skins!"

"Swerg very silly," replied Nick, calmly. "Swerg walk into trap."

Swerg yelped as Nick walked towards him.

"Swerg, listen up! You're a prisoner of war. I need to get to the treasure room, all right? Shiny things."

"Sh-shiny house?" Swerg asked.

"Yes. Take me to the shiny house. Dil Btinid. You can move now, Swerg. But no running off. Understand?"

Swerg gulped, and nodded.

"Good. Now, I don't want to get killed, so take me another way."

"Other way? Swerg not bad goblin. Swerg not let you find out about the secret passage."

"Secret passage?"

"Oh noes! They found out! Nasty pink-skins found out! Swerg bad goblin! Bad!"

"Take us to the passageway, Swerg, or I'll kill you," commanded Nick.

Eve laid a hand on the mage's shoulder. "No, Nick." She turned to Swerg. "Swerg, if you take us to the secret passage, I'll give you this." She lifted a silver dolphin necklace from around her neck, and showed it to the goblin. It was simple yet beautiful, smooth and expertly carved, but above all, it was shiny.

"Oooooh," murmured Swerg. "Shiny." He turned to Nick. "Swerg take you."

"Thank you," muttered Nick, grudgingly.

Thomas gave a cry. Nick's head snapped round. "What is it?"

"It's Alex. He's gone."

Commander Krak'Gragh was angry. The snotties had overwhelmed him, and their little spears were starting to sting. With a roar, he reared up again, and charged from the cavern, crushing slower snotties beneath his iron-shod boots. As he leapt into a tunnel, he turned in the air, and brought his massive fist round against the wall with a stone-breaking crunch. The tunnel shook, and a rain of rocks and dust collapsed down over the entrance, sealing off the cavern and crushing the pursuing snotties. Panting and snorting, he collapsed down onto his haunches.

How? he thought. *How could we lose to a bunch of snotties?*

He was suddenly aware of a sharp object digging into his back. He turned. He was leaning on a human statue. It was a child, by the looks of it. The thing that had been sticking into his back was a stone knife, which the child was holding in both hands. His expression was startled, even afraid.

Krak'Gragh shook himself. There was nothing to fear from a statue. A hiss from behind him interrupted his thoughts. He spun around, snarling, and his heart stopped beating.

"Still no sign of him," observed Nick.

They'd walked over a mile back up the way they had come, but Alex was nowhere to be found. Nick had his staff out, only on its shortened length, desperately casting for a sign of the boy. Suddenly, the staff gave a distant *beep* and he cried out in surprise.

"I've got him. Hardly a trace, but it's there!"

"Which way?" asked Thomas, excitedly.

Nick lifted his head high. "Follow me!"

They hurried down the tunnel, turning left, right, seemingly going in no apparent direction. After a few minutes, the staff beeped again, and Nick turned and began scrabbling at the wall.

"What is it?" asked Eve.

"His magical signature traces right up to this wall. There must be a secret passage."

"I see," said Eve, and joined in with feeling the wall.

Thomas sighed. *We don't have time for this,* he thought. "Stand back!"

Eve and Nick obediently stepped away.

"Hitomas gigantes!" Thomas cried. A blast of white hot fire scorched against the wall, partially melting the stone and shattering the rest. He peered into the smoking ruins.

Standing in front of him was Alex. Or at least, something that resembled Alex.

The Alex that was presented before Thomas was made of grey stone. A solid stone statue.

Nick stepped forward, and scrutinised the carving. "Amazing detail," he commented. "Must have been crafted by a master."

Meanwhile, Eve had found a second statue. It was of an orc. A large, well built orc, tusks spiralling from its lower jaw. Every detail was copied to perfection. In fact it seemed... too perfect.

"Hang on," muttered Nick. "Let me check these statues."

He pointed his staff at the statue of Alex, and it whistled loudly. "That's odd..." he murmured.

"What?" asked Thomas.

"Alex's statue... it shares his magical signature. These statues... were real people."

Swerg poked a statue, and yelped with a sudden fear. He scuttled back, and crouched, quivering and whimpering behind a rock

Nick banged the wall in frustration. "I knew it!" he cried.

"What?"

"How could I have been so... so thick? It's a gorgon!"

"A gorgon?" asked Thomas.

"A gorgon. Tall woman, snakes for hair? Takes the phrase "if looks could kill," far too literally? Come on, haven't you done any Greek mythology?"

"Err..." Thomas dimly recalled a legend about a creature that could turn people to stone. "Medusa?" he offered.

"That's the one! Gorgon queen, caused a hell of a fuss a couple of millennia back. But she wasn't alone, oh no, there are still a load of gorgons alive and kicking in Mythicia."

"Correct," hissed a voice from behind him.

Chapter 18

The Gorgon

Don't turn around!" Nick called warningly. "Not a glimpse. If you see her, you're dead - turned to stone on the spot."

The creature behind him hissed again. "Oh, how clever you are. Thiss one knowss what he'ss dealing with."

"I do," Nick confirmed. "And don't try any of your tricks with me, snake hair, or I'll blast your repulsive head from your shoulders!"

"Ah," said the gorgon. "But to do that, you'll have to look at me, won't you?"

"Not necessarily. A quick fire wave ought to put you out of your misery."

"Ah, you've got me there, I'm afraid. But you wouldn't, would you? You couldn't kill me. I know you, Nicholas. I can ssee your thoughts. You wouldn't kill a creature without even sseeing it. Besidess, you can't move."

"What do you mean?" asked Nick.

"Your armss, your legss, they're freezing up; you can hardly feel them."

She's right¸ thought Nick. *I can't move*.

"Your body iss turning to sstone. You are heavy, sso heavy. Your musscless can't even tense. Nothing will move. Nothing-"

"Leave him alone!" shouted Eve.

"Shut your eyes!" Nick called quickly.

Eve closed her eyes, and a hissing sounded from behind her neck nearly immediately after.

"Ah, little mermaid. Sso protective. You don't want him to die, do you? But you wouldn't choosse him over the human boy, would you?"

"I-I don't know what you're talking about," stuttered Eve.

"But I know you do... Thomass is everything to you, issn't he? You followed him here, because you had *feelingss* for him."

"You-you're lying!"

"Sstill, she denies it. Open your eyess, look at me, and tell me if I am..."

"Don't, Eve!" yelled Thomas. "What ever you do, don't open your eyes!"

"Ignore him!" commanded the gorgon. "He knowss nothing. Uss girlss need to talk. My name is Escalma. And you are Eve. Look at me."

"No!" Eve shouted.

Escalma's voice rose to a high-pitched shriek. "LOOK AT ME!"

Eve couldn't help herself. Her eyes started to open, she had to look-

"Hitomas!" roared Thomas, casting his hand in the direction of the terrible voice. There was a cry, a smell of burning flesh, and the hissing stopped.

Silence reigned. Slowly, ever so slowly, Eve opened her eyes. On the ground in front of her lay a horrifically disfigured face, its eyes burnt beyond recognition. Dead snakes hung from its scalp, some of them still in their death throes. Eve stepped back.

Nick grinned, and slapped Thomas on the back. "Well done," he proclaimed. "You've killed a gorgon. A nasty one at that. Now..." Nick bent down, and plucked a dead snake from the gorgon's scalp. He carried over to the statue of Alex, laid it around his neck. The snake spasmed violently, and the grey started to drain out of Alex and into the snake. Within ten seconds, Alex was a living, breathing boy, and the snake was solid stone. He shuddered, and threw the snake to the floor in disgust, where it shattered into fragments.

"That," Alex said. "Was not pleasant."

"How do you feel?" Nick asked.

"Like a dying rat with indigestion."

"Excellent!" Nick replied. "Everyone says that after they've been petrified. I'll find out why one day! Now," he said, striding over to the gorgon's scorched form. "We won't be needing the body anymore. Shavni!"

A faint breeze swept through the cavern, and the corpse vanished.

"Now," said Nick. "Let's go get that helmet. Swerg!"

The journey was hard, but eventually they managed to scramble back the way they had come. Swerg knew the tunnels like the back of his hand. They changed route several times. "Rockfallses," Swerg explained.

After much scrabbling in the dark, a faint gold light appeared in the distance.

With a new-found energy, they sped towards it, and at last, surfaced from the sea of darkness into...

"Shiny house!" Swerg proclaimed, proudly.

Gold. Everything was gold. Bright light shone off hidden lamps, bouncing and reflecting off the golden armour and transforming into miraculous gold rays. The light hurt Thomas' eyes as he peered into the treasure trove.

"Thank you, Swerg," whispered Eve, lifting the necklace from around her neck, and lowering it over Swerg. If a goblin could blush, Swerg would have done. Swords, armour, goblets, rings and all sorts of precious jewels were strewn across the floor, but raised above the rest, on a colossal podium was...

"The helm!" shouted Nick. "There! The helm of St. George! Thomas, go and get it."

"Why me?" he asked.

"Because you're the Destined and if any of us do it, it'll probably explode or something."

Thomas sighed, and began to scale the mountain of treasure that ringed the podium. As he gripped a golden cup, protruding from the rest, it slid down in his hand with a click.

Nyahhh. Nyahhh. Nyahhh. An alarm began to sound. Slowly, the podium began to sink into the wreckage.

"No!" yelled Thomas, hurriedly scrambling towards it. "Nononononononono!"

He reached out his hand, and grabbed hold of the tip of a feather-like ornament, wielded to the side of the helmet. He pulled, but the helm stuck.

He closed his eyes, and with a voice that came from the depths of his soul, and words that came from some hidden corridor of his mind, he roared. "Eth mai deford! Meot ceom!"

As soon as these strange words had left his mouth, the podium stopped moving, and the helmet rose from its position. It floated towards Thomas, and gently lowered itself over his head.

"Great!" shouted Nick, raising is voice above the din. "Now, let's get the heck out of here."

Thomas jumped from the podium, broke his fall with a roll, and together they sprinted away down the tunnels. Thomas briefly saw Swerg dart right down another tunnel, but said nothing. *Best to let the little guy go*, he thought.

Without any warning, a grey fist swung out from a break-away tunnel, and struck Nick across the face. He collapsed, and the half-life stepped into view.

"Laqsa!" Eve shouted, and the zombie was blown off its feet by a blast of water.

Nick stepped forward again, but the creature grabbed his foot with inhuman strength. He tried to shake it free, but the half-life refused to relax its grip. It slowly rose to its feet, its own arm twisting at an impossible angle.

"Hitomas!" the mage yelled, pushing his hand into the creature's face. Flames billowed out around the thing's decaying head, burning the hideous face into an unorganised mess. And yet, even as its face crackled with flame, still it held on.

"Run!" shouted Nick. Thomas turned, but another half-life was blocking his path. Its face twisted into a grin.

"...no...escape" it rasped. "... surrender..."

Nick turned his head. "That's it!" he declared. "We surrender!"

"What?" asked Thomas, incredulous.

"Trust me!" replied Nick, wincing as the half-life's grip tightened.

They all raised their arms, except for Nick, who raised his free hand.

"Oh... yes!" cried a voice. The ceiling above them split, and a beam of hot white light shone through. Then, it exploded, raining ash and soil down on the group below. Raiza descended, floating on the air and laughing maniacally.

"At last, The Destined, the Mage, the Mermaid and the Apprentice, all assembled together. You wouldn't believe the trouble you've caused. But it matters not. Now, you are in my custody. Any questions?"

The rebels glared up at the demonic figure.

"What happened to your voice?" asked Alex.

"My voice?" asked the gruesome apparition. *"This was always my voice. If it is the child's voice you're referring to, however, then I believe it is best for me to tell the truth. The one who called himself Raiza is gone."*

"Gone?" asked Nick.

"Correct, mortal. His body is mine, and his mind is cast into the nether realms. He is gone. There is only me..."

"Then who are you?" Thomas shouted.

"I am the beginning and the end. I am the Alpha, and the Omega. I am the all, and the only. I am the rise, and the Fall."

"What kind of an answer is that?" Thomas retorted.

"One full of riddles and secrets. Don't think your pathetic attempts to stall for time will work on me."

"It was worth a try..." conceded Nick.

"Your time is up. Now, the Destined shall come with me. But only the Destined. The rest of you are expendable, and will be killed." The creature in Raiza's body clicked its fingers. *"Half-lifes!"* he roared. *"Put these worms out of their misery."*

The zombies stepped forward, arms outstretched in a life-ending embrace.

"Wait!" Eve called. The half-lifes stopped.

"Begging for mercy, sea dweller?"

"You should be!" the mermaid yelled. "Laqsa!"

Her hands shot forward, and a foaming blast of water shot towards the floating Raiza. He smiled, held up his hand, and the water turned to ice in the air. It paused for a moment, defying gravity as Raiza studied it. And then, with a casual flick of his wrist, he sent it smashing to the ground with a crash.

"Pathetic..." Raiza murmured. *"For that, I might just spare you. It will be interesting to see what Malcaractimus has in store for you."*

Chapter 19

The Method in the Madness

It was dark in the cargo hold of the *Emperor's Wrath*. Very dark. It was also cold. So cold that Thomas could almost feel his blood turning to ice. He shivered. Raiza had taken them up to his ship, the others had been dragged away from him, and Thomas had been hurled into this pit. *If Hell ever freezes over*, thought Thomas, *it would be exactly like this*.

Someone had taken his sword and helm. Whoever it was was going to pay some time soon.

The room shook violently, and Thomas rolled to the opposite wall. He bounced a few times, and groaned as his knee cracked threateningly. There was a dull thump, and the room seemed to settle. They must have landed. He had to hand it to Raiza – the engine was completely silent. There was a *ding* and some hidden door slid open, revealing a patch of white light.

A demon that looked human from the waist up slithered inside. It was able to slither, because its bottom half was that of a snake. Long and thin, it ended in an arrow-shaped point, barbed and glistening with venom. The creature was holding a three pointed trident in both hands, each of its prongs ending in cruel hooks.

"You..." it rasped. "You... Destined. You will... come."

It prodded Thomas with its trident. Thomas considered killing it with a spell, but where would he go? He supposed he'd better follow this demon, and see where it took him.

He rose to his feet, and followed the demon out into the square of light. It opened into a hexagonal metal corridor. Flashing red and purple lights illuminated the tube, and odd black circuit boxes hung down from the ceiling and walls.

At the end of the corridor was a pitch-black door. Staring at it for more than a few seconds made Thomas feel dizzy. It seemed to suck him in, draining him of life. The snake demon punched a code into a pad beside the door, and it slid open.

Raiza was seated in a similarly dark throne, slouching nonchalantly across an arm. He smiled as Thomas was marched in.

"Ah, the Destined. I trust you had a pleasant journey?"

"Yeah," replied Thomas, sarcastically. "The room service was a bit slow, though."

"Yes, I can see it gives you pleasure to chide me. But I also see through your laughter. You are terrified. You have every reason to be. But the real terror is yet to come. This way!"

Raiza rose from his chair, and another two snake-demons slunk over to Thomas. They prodded him forward with their tridents. There was a faint mechanical whirr, and the entire wall behind the malevolent entity slid away, revealing the planet they had landed on.

"Behold!" the thing possessing Raiza proclaimed. *"The great city of Odmehlwor!"*

The first thing that struck Thomas was the smell. A foul, sickening smell of decay. It smelt like death. Stretching out before Thomas was a once-magnificent city. Hundreds of years ago, it must have been beautiful. Today, it was horrific.

Where mighty towers had once touched the sky, only blackened ruins remained. Homely cottages had become shadowy hovels. The streets that were once paved with gold now seemed to be pasted with black, stinking mud.

And all through the shattered and broken wreckage, scurried nearly infinite multitudes of demons. Hundreds of thousands of the hideous creatures filled the streets and buildings, and all chanting one phrase:

"THE DESTINED COMES! MALCARACTIMUS RISES!

THE DESTINED COMES! MALCARACTIMUS RISES!

THE DESTINED COMES! MALCARACTIMUS RISES!

FEAR OUR LORD!"

The fearsome chant carried on, and on, echoing across the stricken landscape. It filled every corner, every nook, every cranny. It bellowed across the entire planet.

With an ear-piercing scream, Thomas collapsed, and let unconsciousness take him.

Back on the *Wrath*, Nicholas the Wise opened his eyes. So far so good. He lay there, deadly still, calculating his next move. He was in pitch darkness. That could mean he was blind, or it could mean he was in a room without light. Well, he could soon fix that.

"Lhigbort." The darkness shrank back as the tiny orb of light shimmered into the air, allowing Nick to take stock of his surroundings. Well, it proved he wasn't blind after all, which was a relief.

He was in some sort of cell. Presumably, he was still on the ship, and with any luck, so were Alex and Eve. They would have taken Thomas as soon as they landed, he was certain of that.

The mage examined himself. They'd left him with his robes, so at least he had his dignity, but as for his staff, he hadn't been so lucky. He patted his pockets, hopefully. Strictly speaking, he didn't *need* the staff, but it certainly helped channel his magic. He stood up, just to stretch his legs. By the gods, they were stiff. Mythicia was host to a nigh-on infinite number of religions, each with their own array of gods, but Nick didn't really belong to any of them. He preferred to pick and choose the gods he thought he liked, and it seemed to have worked so far. That said, he could really use with some divine help right now.

The cell was square and barren, with no visible doorway. If there had been, he would have tried to pick it open, either physically or with magic, but his captors had naturally thought of that. The only thing for it was to sit and see what Raiza had in store for him.

He didn't have to wait long. After what felt like minutes, a square of light appeared in the wall, and standing in it was a lean yet menacing silhouette.

"And here you are!" the mage exclaimed with a smile. "How can I help you?"

The figure took two long strides forward, seizing Nick's shoulders roughly with two firm but noticeably elven hands. It hauled the mage back through the square of light and into a corridor, where it turned and dragged Nick stumbling behind it. In the glow of the dim electric lights that lined the tunnel, he saw his jailor was clothed in robes like his, only utterly black. That in itself set bells ringing somewhere in his memory, and looking up, he saw the elf's hair was tied in a black ponytail. He tried to stop then and there, but his captor was stronger than he was, dragging him on, through an open door and out into the searing light of day.

At this point, a sack was shoved over his head from behind, blinding him as he was pulled onwards. The stone ground tore at his knees and shins, ripping the skin and soaking his lower robes with blood. Nick hissed through his clenched teeth, trying not to give his captor the satisfaction of a cry. Then he was lifted up and thrown onto some sort of wooden platform. The sound of wheels over rock and the feel of momentum suggested he was now in the back of a cart. Weakly, he scrambled across the floor, the elf still keeping a firm grip on his robes. The mage's scrabbling fingers found the barrier at the back of the cart, and he lent against it.

"You're unusually quiet," he said through the sack.

"You recognise me then?" The reply was cold, empty of emotion.

"Of course. Given all the work we did together it would be rude of me not to."

The elf snorted. "You speak as though we were friends."

"Well we were. Or at least I considered you a friend. Even after you did what you did."

Nick's captor remained silent.

"Why the sack, Rallen? You always had more style than this."

The elf chuckled.

"What's the joke?" Nick asked.

"I haven't heard that name in years."

"What, going by your other name again? I have to say, it broke my heart to hear you'd gone back to what I thought we'd saved you from."

A hand grabbed hold of Nick's neck and snapped his head forward. Through the sack, he could feel hot breath on his face, as his captor's voice whispered into his ear.

"Saved me? By 'saving me' you took away the only power I ever had. My only Discipline and you tricked me into abandoning it. And why?

Because of morality. Well now I know better, Nicholas the *Wise*. Now I know necromancy isn't something to bury, to hide from the light. Now I know how *glorious* the Death Discipline is," here, he gave a harsh bark of laughter. "You claim such superiority, call yourself "the Wise!" How wise was it of you to fall for such a simple trap of mine? We knew you would bring the Destined to Atlantis, so I made plans. The red pads, the helm, it was all designed to lure you to Panoga, where the Fall and his pet gorgon captured you. The plan was mine, but do I get any credit? No. But then again, I hardly need it. I have you at my mercy, mage, and believe me, revenge is oh so much sweeter than any credit the Emperor could give me."

The sack was ripped from Nick's head as he stared into the fierce green eyes of the elf he used to know. "'Rallen' died when I left our petty trio behind. My name is Valcoz now, and you will do well to remember it."

Nick sighed. "How could I forget it?" The cart jolted to a halt, and the mage looked up, at the skies of Odmehlwor and the mighty, towering prison block that blotted out half of the horizon. "Well?" he said. "Shall we go in?"

Thomas woke to the sound of laughter. Or at least he thought it was laughter. It was either laughter, or someone being brutally throttled. *Probably laughter*¸ Thomas thought.

He grudgingly opened his eyes. Filling his vision was an upside down snake-demon. Raiza stood beside him, also upside down. Then, Thomas' brain cells sorted themselves out, and then he realized that it was in fact he who was upside down. Realizing this, he screamed.

“Shut up, and stand up,” someone said.

Thomas stood up. Raiza and the snake-demon turned themselves the right way up. All three of them were illuminated in a bright light, surrounded completely by utter darkness.

“Move,” commanded a deep voice, echoing out of the shadows. Thomas started to move-

“Not you, mortal! I meant the guard and my brother.”

The snake demon disappeared. Raiza smiled menacingly, and left the room. Thomas squinted into the darkness. Only the sound of steadily approaching claws clicking on the hard floor penetrated the silence. Thomas gasped as a tall, hulking, demonic creature stood silhouetted at the edge of spotlight – a dark tower of malice and wrath.

“Who are you?” asked Thomas.

“Can’t you guess?” the beastly apparition replied.

Thomas tried to open his mouth to quip something back, but an indomitable feeling of dread locked around his vocal cords and pinned his tongue behind his teeth.

The strange laugh/strangle sounded again.

“My name is Malcaractimus. I rule Mythicia. Which means I also rule you, Destined.”

At this Thomas overcame his terror just enough for a moment’s defiance. “You might “rule me,” but you don’t frighten me. You’re not even brave enough to show your face.”

“Silence!” roared the demon lord. In a heartbeat, the demon burst into view, leaping into the light. His skin was red, blue veins pulsing across his neck and chest. His leathery wings flapped indignantly, and his long, sword-like claws slashed through the air. Two razor sharp horns curled from his skull, but the most terrifying thing about him was his eyes. They were black. Not just his irises, but the entire eyeball was a pure, void black. Like the gate and Raiza's throne, the demon's eyes seemed to suck Thomas' soul from his body.

"I am your lord, and you *will* obey me. Learn some respect." *Click, click*, went his claws as he approached Thomas' quivering form. The demon levelled his face with his, so close that Thomas could smell nothing but the rancid meat on his breath.

"Kneel" the emperor whispered.

And part of Thomas wanted to kneel, to let the demon do whatever he wanted with him without a fight, to give himself up. But that would be letting the demon win.

"No," he breathed, and the part that wanted to surrender screamed at his audacity. Wordlessly, Malcaractimus lifted Thomas by the scruff of his neck up high into the air. He slowly and precisely lifted a claw, and drew a long slit across Thomas' arm. Thomas winced as the blood oozed.

"I could kill you in a second, mortal," the demon said, quietly. "But I won't. The Destined must not be killed. Not until the Night of the Black Star. You will be executed with the whole of Odmehlwor assembled before you. My demons shall watch you die, and you will realise your ultimate purpose. But first!" the demon grinned, revealing a two rows of sharp white teeth. "I think you deserve an explanation." He turned away, clicking back across the light.

Thomas couldn't wait any longer. Now was his chance. Thomas made a run at the demon, the words of a spell forming on his lips, but two snake-demons leapt out from the shadows and held him back. Thomas struggled, but his captors held him firm, their sharp nails forming a row of miniature crescents on his arms.

"You see, mortal," began Malcaractimus turning back to face him.

"Your world is a waste of space. It is a universe populated only by swarms of idiotic *humans*. You scurry from place to place, like ants in a nest, like bees from a hive. You then destroy each other in wars, and most of which are fought over ridiculous purposes such as some strange *religion*. You fight over which "God" you think exists, which fiction you think protects you. *Fools!* If there were a God, why does he let people fall ill and die? Why does he let you feel pain? Why does he allow misery? Face it - he doesn't exist. The only God in either universe is *me*!"

"You're not a God!" protested Thomas. "What power do you have over my race? None! You're stuck here in Mythicia, unable to even enter my universe! You can't break that law; no one can!"

"Please understand, Mr Colfrey. I don't *need* your universe. You are everything I require."

"What?"

"Soon, I will have more power than any God and you're about to find out why," to his guard, he added, "Take him!"

The guards seized Thomas, and marched him through a large metal gate and into an incredibly curious room. It was large, square, and metal, and in the centre of it stood a circle of stones, not unlike the one Thomas had travelled through in Atlantis. However, these stones were black, as black as the darkest night, and Thomas realised they were made of the same substance the gate and Raiza's throne had been made of.

"It's a Monolith Gate," Thomas whispered, realisation dawning on him. "But where will you go?"

Malcaractimus grinned, revealing two rows of sharpened fangs. "Nowhere. You are correct in seeing it as a Monolith Gate, but it is also far more."

The Emperor began to pace up and down the circle.

"Once every hundred thousand years, an incredible magical phenomenon takes place. It is known as the Night of the Black Star. On this night, Alpha Negasia, the brightest star in Mythicia, turns black. I'm sure Nicholas told you of the prophecy concerning you, but very few in this universe know of the second prophecy. It runs like this:

The Fall and the Destined, a broken lord.

The Destined's blade, an Ancient's sword.

The Fall will be felled, the Tears will restore.

The End will draw near, as it happened before.

In-"

Thomas cut the demon off, the words he had heard when he saved Nick from the trolls suddenly flooding back to him:

"the Black Star's Shadow, in the circle of stones,

The Fall and the Destined, before the Throne of Bones,

Can release the Old Darkness, and break the last seal,

And all of Creation before the Dragon shall kneel."

Malcaractimus froze, and stared at Thomas. "How do you know those words?" he whispered.

"They came to me when I was travelling through a Monolith Gate. Why?"

"That should not be possible. But in the end it means nothing. The meaning of the prophecy is clear to me. When the Black Star appears, its dark light will shine directly onto this stone circle. You and the Fall will both be in the circle, and then "the Dragon" shall arrive. I will bend it to my will, and then I will have the power of a god!"

Thomas shivered. This was bad, bad news. But there was one thing he didn't quite understand. "Who's the Fall?" he asked.

"Don't you know?" Malcaractimus asked, chuckling mockingly. "The Fall is the mortal you knew as Raiza."

"And Raiza's under your control..."

"Precisely. And now, you are too. You will be made to stand in the circle with him."

"What if I refuse?"

"Then you will know more pain than you could ever have imagined."

Malcaractimus chuckled, and the demon's form seemed to rise and grow before Thomas' eyes, engulfing all his vision.

"In two orbits of Lunadraxis 5 – that's approximately six months in human reckoning – the Black Star will rise, and the Dragon's power will be mine!"

Malcaractimus threw back his head, and roared with maniacal laughter, which echoed across the hall, rebounding again and again with more and more vigour.

"The rebels will stop you!" Thomas shouted, and the demon stopped laughing, staring right into his eyes. The area inside the circle darkened, and Thomas felt as if his very life was being drained from his body. He jerked, and fell back into nothing.

Chapter 21

Escape

When Thomas awoke, he found himself in another dark and cold cell. This time, he had been provided with a bench, but that was all. No doors or windows were visible, but two faint blue lamps gave off what little light there was.

His stomach rumbled, and the familiar pang of hunger told him he needed food. He was somehow glad – it was the only thing here he knew. As if by magic, and Thomas realised it probably was, a bowl of black porridge dropped out of the air in front of him and onto the floor with a clink.

He crawled forward, prodded the bowl. There was no spoon, but Thomas didn't care – he was so hungry nothing mattered anymore. He lifted the bowl to his lips, and sipped the black porridge.

It was cold, and tasted foul. At the first sip, Thomas gagged and wretched, placing the bowl back on the ground. No matter how hungry he was, he couldn't eat that.

As if on cue, the bowl vanished, and Thomas was left alone in the cell. He had to get out of here. He had to get out, and rescue Nick, Alex and Eve. He began to slowly search the walls and floor. It was hopeless, he knew, but it was worth a try. There had to be something that could aid his escape. Something.

His heart leapt as his fingers latched themselves over a ledge of some sort. Upon close inspection, Thomas deemed it to be a grill in the floor. It was about as wide as his head and shoulders, and if he could somehow remove it, he would be able to pull himself through.

A heavy metal bolt secured the grill in place. He managed to get his fingers round one of them. With a silent prayer to any god or deity who might be listening, he closed his eyes and pulled. There was a click and the grill came free.

Impossible! There was no way he alone could have broken the bolt. He peered down into the gloom below, and something wet and sticky struck him across the face.

Thomas yelped, and backed away, as a reddish-pink, dripping figure lurched out of the hole the grill had covered. It reached towards Thomas, who pushed himself as far into the corner as he could manage.

"Thomas!" whispered the reddish pink creature, urgently.

"Who... what...who are you?" Thomas whispered back, shaking.

The figure wiped some of the reddish pink off his face, revealing it to be a strange sticky goo. "I'm Nick, stupid!" the figure whispered. "It's not pretty down there, I can tell you, but it's an escape."

Thomas whimpered. "I don't believe you."

"Come on, I'm here to rescue you!" The figure tried to whisper and shout at the same time. It failed.

Thomas decided to trust this thing. After all, what else could he do? "Fine," he said. "If you really are Nick, I'll come with you."

"Brilliant," sighed Nick. "Come on!"

Nick crawled back to the hole, and dropped down. There was a splash below. Thomas peered down.

"It's alright!" Nick called.

"What is that stuff?" Thomas asked, seeing a river of the reddish pink stuff flowing beneath him.

"Would you believe me if I said it was strawberry milkshake?" Nick tried.

"No."

"Fair enough."

There was an awkward silence.

"What is it?" Thomas insisted.

There was another silence. "This is a sewer, Thomas."

"So that's demon..."

"Yep. Lovely, isn't it? Come on."

Thomas closed his eyes, and jumped down the hole. The goo was surprisingly warm, and squidgy. He struggled through it to Nick, who was treading water. Well, treading goo.

"This way!"

Nick sort of swam through the gunk and down the tunnel through which the pink stuff flowed. Thomas followed him, spitting out goo. It did taste of strawberry milkshake.

Further down the tunnel, Nick pulled himself onto a sort of ledge, and went through an open door. Thomas dislodged himself from the goo, and followed him.

It led to stone dome of a room, where a fire roared, illuminating Alex and Eve. Nick slumped down next to them. Thomas squelched in after him.

"Thomas!" exclaimed Alex, who ran forward to hug him, but thought better of it. He didn't like the idea of a strawberry milkshake coat.

"Right," began Nick. "There's no time to lose. Now we've got Thomas, we need to get out of here. Immediately!" He looked down at his clothes. "Or at least, as soon as I've got rid of this goo..."

At this point in time, up in the palace above, Malcaractimus was raging.

"HOW?" he roared, "How could you let him escape?" He glared around the room at the assembled demons. "This is quite possibly the most pathetic sight I've ever seen in my life!" There was silence. "Who was in charge of the Destined's cell?"

A six legged demon tentatively raised a tentacle. "M-m-me, l-lord..."

Malcaractimus leapt upon the creature, his claws flailing. Silence reigned as the cowering demon was torn to shreds.

Wiping his claws on a wing, Malcaractimus struggled for control over himself. "Now," he began. "I want everything we have, and I *mean* everything, scouring this planet for the boy! And I do *not* want to see you fail. *You* do not want me to see you fail. I can make your life a living hell. Understand? I want to see the Destined's body broken before me before the day is out! Or there will be consequences..."

The demon trailed off, leaving a hint of menace hovering in the air. A demon coughed. Malcaractimus glared at it with such rage in his eyes that the creature whimpered.

"Do not fail me..." the demon lord whispered.

Thomas pushed the manhole aside, wincing as a shaft of brilliant daylight lanced down into the tunnel. He climbed out into the demon city, glanced around, and dropped back down to the others.

"All clear," he called. Nick, Alex and Eve climbed up behind him. They hurried out across the road, and darted into the shadows as a demon patrol marched past.

There were thirteen of them in total, all hideous amalgamations of claws, teeth and tentacles, scuttling and slithering across the roads. They didn't seem to have a visible leader, but Thomas wouldn't have recognised one even if they did – each monster seemed completely unique amongst the rest.

"Malcaractimus has got his troops out in force," observed Nick. "We've got to be careful."

Nick had explained the plan to Thomas before they left.

"When we came off the ship, we landed in a docking bay," Nick had explained. "I saw four or five other ships there. If we can find our way back there, we'll be fine."

Thomas had asked: "How did you get down into the sewers?"

"When they threw us in the cell," Nick had said, "They didn't consider me casting a doorstop spell."

"What?"

"A doorstop spell. Literally a magical little stopper that sits under the doorframe. Kept it open a crack. My jailor and I go back a long way, so luckily for me his gloating stopped him noticing."

An hour later, they had come up from the sewers and were sneaking through the streets towards the docking bay. Thomas stuck a head out from behind a column. "They're gone," he whispered.

Nick leading, they tiptoed from shadow to shadow through the streets, until the vast metal monolith that was the docking bay came into view. A sign told them the "arrivals" area was on the ground floor, but the "departures" was on the top. They would have to climb the tower, and find a ship at the top.

Nick marched up to a pair of sliding doors at the foot of the tower, and pushed on them hands. When there was no response, he pushed again, harder, and smacked his staff against the glass. It bounced off, jarring his wrist.

Nick swore, and retreated back into the shadows. "Must've set it up to only open for demons," he explained. He started muttering a spell, but Eve touched his arm. "You don't have to," she whispered. "Look." Nick looked, and the doors slid open. He raised his eyebrows, and stepped out, but at that moment a burly scorpion-like demon emerged from the building. It was a man from the waist up, but in place of its legs were a series of armoured legs, tiny bone points clicking across the concrete. A menacing tail curved from its back, ending in a cruel sting above its head.

It saw Nick and grinned, revealing inhumanly sharp and pointed teeth. And then, in the blink of an eye, it was on him, lashing out with its poison coated tail. The mage brought his staff up only just in time, but he had to spin it like a helicopter blade to keep up with the strokes.

"We have to do something," hissed Thomas.

"We can't," replied Alex. "If we distract Nick in the slightest, that thing will kill him."

"But we can't just sit here and do *nothing*," Thomas whispered back.

"No, you're right. We can't. But what *can* we do?"

He glanced around behind him, and begun scanning the surroundings furiously.

"Where's Eve?" he asked, urgently.

At that moment, the scorpion creature flicked Nick's staff out of his hands with its tail, sending it bouncing along the ground. The demon leered over the stricken mage, its eyes searing with triumph.

Someone shouted, and it was thrown up high into the air, a blast of water propelling it into space. It screeched, hovering in the air for a moment, and then it came crashing down to the road below, its limbs splaying at impossible angles. Thomas winced.

Eve popped out from behind a column, smiling. Nick unsteadily pulled himself to his feet. "Thank you," he murmured to Eve. "You saved my life."

"You're welcome," she replied. "But we still need to get in that door."

"I think," began Nick, dusting himself down. "That problem no longer exists."

He picked up his staff, and swung it down on the dead demon's leg. Black blood spewed from the corpse, and the armoured leg broke free of the evil torso. Nick picked it up, and tapped it against the doors, which slid open, the computerised voice greeting them. "Welcome, Korsmarg," it intoned.

Thomas laughed quietly to himself. "Nice one."

"Thanks," Nick replied.

They strode through the doors, and into the building itself. It opened up into a circular room, no doors or windows presenting themselves. “That’s funny,” muttered Alex.

Then, the doors closed behind them, and red light filled the small space. Suddenly, Thomas felt a sensation of rising. He glanced at Nick. “Can you feel that?” he asked.

Nick opened his mouth to reply, but the words were ripped from his lips as the entire party was thrown, as one, to the ground. Thomas’ stomach threatened to leap out of his mouth. The room was flying up the tower at a terrific pace. Eve screamed.

Just as suddenly as it had begun, the rising stopped. Once Thomas’ internal organs had put themselves back in the correct places, he stood up. The doors slid open with a *ding*, and the docking station opened up before them.

Nick pointed to a suitable ship. “That’s our ticket out of here,” he explained. “Alex, if you’d do the honours...”

Alex reached up and touched the ship. It was long and black, its name stated in glittering red letters across the hull. *Black River*. Alex started muttering quietly: “Heworit purouy emin.”

The ship shimmered, and a door opened in its side. Alex climbed in, and the others followed. Sleek leather seats lined the interior, and white lights shone down from the ceiling.

Nick wandered to the front, and spotted a wheel and pedals opposite one of the seats. He sat down. “Everyone strapped in?” he called. There was a series of affirmative grunts. “Good!” he said. “Let’s go!”

Chapter 22

Raiza's Vengeance

The ship shot off into the air, trailing a cloud of black smoke in its wake. Thomas was thrown back against his seat, his cheeks rippling like a miniature ocean. After a few minutes, the ship stabilized, and Thomas stopped feeling like the inside of a vacuum cleaner.

A thin reedy voice crackled through a concealed speaker somewhere on the ship. "Ship *Black River*, please identify. Repeat, please identify. You are attempting an unauthorised departure from the planet's vicinity."

Nick grinned in the pilot seat, and ignored the voice.

"You will not be warned again. Please identify."

Nick hit a button, and the voice shut off. Thomas relaxed. They'd escaped. They were safe. He breathed a sigh of relief.

A terrifying thud shook the ship. Thomas jolted forward in his seat. There was another crash, and the ship shook again. "We're losing altitude!" shouted Nick.

There was a great screeching and rending of metal, and a black, bloodstained claw ripped through the wall just inches above Thomas' head. He screamed, and Alex hurled a fireball at the claw, but it exploded without leaving so much as a scorch mark. Alex looked at the hand he'd used to throw the fire in surprise.

"Sensors indicate a large object attached to the side of the ship!" called Nick.

"You don't say?" Thomas called back, ripping off his seatbelt and leaping across the cabin.

There was another crash, and a second claw smashed through the wall. Together, the two menacing hands ripped the metal apart, revealing Malcaractimus' grinning face.

"Here, little piggies..." the demon called, mockingly, yet oh so hungrily.

Eve screamed, and Alex leapt away from the opening.

The demon widened the gap and reached into the ship with a claw, seizing hold of Thomas' ankle. He howled in pain as the knife-sharp nails ripped into foot, but Malcaractimus only laughed, pulling Thomas out of the ship and casting the stricken vessel aside. As soon as he had done so, the demon twisted Thomas round in the air to watch as the *Black River* plummeted from the sky and smashed against the docking tower, which in turn crumpled to the ground. With a titanic *"whoosh!"* a great cloud of fire mushroomed up from the wreckage, blazing against the sky with such heat that Thomas could feel it on his skin even this far away. He screamed again, as Malcaractimus beat his wings and soared across the sky, clutching Thomas in a gruesome claw.

Thomas struggled, and then thought better of it. If Malcaractimus dropped him now, the fall would certainly kill him. He had to try to force the demon to land. He closed his eyes, and a passage of True Speak he had never heard before formed inside his mind. "Meot ceom, drows ghiloft," he whispered, and his sword was suddenly in his hand. He lifted it above his head, and gauged a long slice of flesh out of Malcaractimus' wing. Black blood spattered from the wound as the blade ripped through the leathery skin and the demon cried out, bringing Thomas up level with his eyes.

"Do not strike me again, mortal," he intoned, his eyes blazing with rage, his breath hot against Thomas' face. "Do not strike me again, or I will crush the life from your body."

"No!" Thomas shouted over the howling wind, desperation mingling with defiance. "You can't kill me, because then you won't have me on the night of the Black Star!"

"Correct. However, I can put you through agony of the like a child such as yourself could not hope to comprehend."

Thomas pulled himself together, gathered up all the courage he could muster, and swung his sword at Malcaractimus' face. The demon howled in pain, spitting more foul-smelling blood into Thomas' eyes, and dropped from the sky, plummeting towards the black wastelands of Odmehlwor. At the last moment, he spread his wings, and the descent slowed, the demon alighting gently on the ebony soil.

"You..." the emperor growled, clutching his bloody face with one claw and throwing Thomas to the ground with the other. "You have tried my patience."

He raised a bladed digit, and Thomas' confidence deserted him as he realised Malcaractimus was angry enough to kill him where he stood. He screamed, and flattened himself to the ground, wishing it could swallow him up and take him away from this madness.

And then, his feelings changed. Fear turned to anger, nerves turned to confidence, and flight...

Turned to retribution.

It could not end like this.

Thomas rose. His body spun upright, and there he stood, facing the demon emperor and laughing in his face.

Dimly, in the back of his mind, he knew this was the Bloodrage. He knew this wasn't him. But it was beyond his control now, and it was what he needed to survive. And looking into the demon's eyes, he realised Malcaractimus knew it too.

"I wish it had not come to this," the emperor growled. "But your Bloodrage has made you too great a threat."

Thomas stared back at the demon, holding his gaze. "I know."

And those were all the words that were necessary. In perfect synchrony, boy and demon stepped towards each other. Thomas flourished his sword, Malcaractimus raised a claw.

The sound of claw on steel shattered the silence of the wastelands, as two lone figures grappled with each other, not over desire for power or glory, but over the desire to live. Malcaractimus tore at Thomas' clothes and skin, and Thomas's blade stabbed again and again into the demon's flesh. But both fighters were imbued with magic beyond understanding, and their wounds healed and healed again. The Bloodrage had made Thomas almost invincible, but even so, Malcaractimus would not be beaten.

Adrenaline pumped, blood spattered, anger rose and ebbed like a tide. After what seemed like a lifetime, they broke apart, staggering metres away from each other. After a second's pause, the battle turned magical. The Bloodrage released Thomas from the bonds of True Speak; it made him a master of magic in its pure, uncontrolled form. But he had to make this quick – already he could feel its fury weakening.

Lightning flashed and fire sparked, the ground itself split around the combatants, locked together at the eye of the magical storm. To an onlooker, it would have seemed as though the forces of nature themselves had taken up arms and gone to do battle, and perhaps, in a sense, they had. But onlookers there were not. Just the two.

Malcaractimus and Thomas stared into each other's eyes as the elements whirled around them. The Destined and the Emperor, matched almost perfectly in power. But not quite in skill. Thomas was a mere child, Malcaractimus had lived for hundreds of years – all that experience gave him a mastery over magic Thomas had yet to understand. Because of that, and because his Bloodrage was wearing off, Thomas slowly began to realise that he was losing.

He started to back away, keeping up a barrage of the magic that simply came to him, but Malcaractimus pushed forward. He couldn't give in, not now, not yet, it couldn't be so. Even as he tried desperately to renew his assault, something changed in the battle. The storm ceased to be a two-way struggle; a third force pushed down from above. Thomas looked up, and everything went dark.

It lasted only for half a second, but when the shadows cleared, Raiza stood between Malcaractimus and Thomas, and the Bloodrage left him.

"I see you have recovered the Destined, brother," the possessed boy observed.

Malcaractimus, stunned for a moment, rallied magnificently. "I have, as you will do well to observe. The boy will not escape again, but I would appreciate it if you could accompany me back to the stronghold."

Raiza grinned, and a strange light flickered in his eyes.

"Oh, you're not going back to your stronghold, emperor..." he whispered.

"What?" asked Malcaractimus. Thomas was equally confused.

"You will be going on a... different journey." As Raiza said this, he raised his hand in the demon-lord's direction. *"Neothilican telebrik!"* Some primeval instinct made Thomas hurl himself to one side, just as a bolt of black lightning streaked towards the demon overlord, striking him in the chest and knocking him to the ground.

In an eye-blink, Malcaractimus was back on his feet. "How dare you?" he seethed. "After all we've done together, how dare you betray me? Hathingbarik!"

The demon's eyes flashed gold, and a pillar of rock streaked upwards from the ground behind Raiza, collapsing onto the boy like a tumbling mountain. "*Garithol!*" he screeched before the rocks struck him, and with a flash of darkness, he was suddenly beside the demon, one arm round his neck.

Malcaractimus twisted, and not bothering to use any magic at all, ripped a claw across Raiza's face. Blood flowed freely, and the boy loosened his grip, staggering backwards. Even as he healed the damage with frantic words, Malcaractimus loomed over him, striking down with a deadly sweep-

"*Btind*" Raiza whispered.

Malcaractimus froze, his entire body caught mid-movement. Only his eyes continued to move, frantically flickering left and right. Thomas scrambled across the black dust, and ducked behind a rock. He peered round, watching the scene.

Raiza smiled. "*Troemnt,*" he whispered again. Malcaractimus flung out his arms and legs in a star shape, and began to spasm madly and furiously, writhing in unimaginable agony. His hands and feet shook, his eyes rolled, his head lolled, and his mouth opened in a silent scream. Thomas recoiled, disgusted by the display.

Raiza grinned, watching Malcaractimus with delight. He laughed, and after a few minutes, spoke a single word.

"*Escarek.*"

And thus, Malcaractimus, demon emperor of all Mythica, fell limp, and ceased to live.

Raiza raised his head. His eyes focused on the rock Thomas was cowering behind.

"It's no use hiding, Destined," Raiza called. *"I see you. I smell your fear. Come out!"*

Thomas quivered, and flattened himself against the rock.

"I ask you again, Thomas Colfrey. Come out!"

Still Thomas remained behind the rock, paralysed with fear.

"*Meot ceom!*" Raiza roared.

Thomas suddenly felt himself stand up, and his legs walked him towards Raiza of their own accord.

"Now Thomas Colfrey. Now you will die, and I will return to Malcaractimus' stronghold, where I will assume his mantle of emperor. But first, there is a more important task to complete."

Thomas felt Raiza release him from the spell. "Why did you kill him?" he asked.

Raiza laughed. *"His usefulness had reached its end. He had become an obstacle. As have his demons. And as the Fall, I have the power to remove them."*

"What?"

"The demonic race is putrid. Ugly. Unclean. I have the power of the Fall, and that combined with my own strength allows me to wipe away their filth in the name of purity!"

Raiza raised his hand, and a black disc materialised in the air before Thomas. It shimmered and grew, and slowly, fading out of the darkness, an image of Malcaractimus' city emerged. Thousands of demons swarmed across the streets, pouring in and out of the ruins.

"Before you lies the largest gathering of demons in all creation. What you are about to see will be happening all over the universe. The demons have infested Mythicia, and now I..." He waved a hand. *"-Will exterminate them with a few words. Aerse mesehtond mroftemi sefilt."*

As he spoke, his eyes glinted, and every demon in the image

suddenly began to fade, the colour draining from their bodies before the grey husks themselves crumbled to dust.

Thomas glanced across at the body of Malcaractimus. It too was rotting away, consumed by Raiza's spell.

Suddenly, he felt an inexplicable sense of forgetfulness, as if something hugely important had slipped from his mind. He dismissed it - he had more important things to think about, like how Raiza had caused the disappearance of... of what? The demons... no, what were demons? No, he had to remember, he had to, he couldn't let them slip from his memory, he had to...

He blacked out.

The blackout only lasted a second, but it felt like a lifetime. Raiza caught Thomas with an outstretched hand as he fell. The moment had passed. He suddenly remembered where he was. He had to get away from Raiza. Thomas jerked out of his grasp, and ran as fast as his legs could carry him, but Raiza simply darted forward, and seized him by the throat.

"Goodbye, Thomas Colfrey," he whispered, and tightened his grip.

Chapter 23

An Unseen Battle

Raiza squeezed Thomas' throat, tighter and tighter. Thomas felt his very breath being crushed from his lungs. He couldn't breathe, he couldn't think, he couldn't even see properly. A terrifying blackness was creeping form the corners of his eyes, spreading across his vision like some dark parasite. He would have screamed, but he had no breath to scream with. He was dying, and he knew it.

He stared at Raiza's face, the twisted visage smiling with grim satisfaction. His green eyes were burning with hatred, the irises themselves flickering like flames. Raiza laughed, each harsh syllable breaking through whatever confidence Thomas had left.

The creeping darkness had practically blinded Thomas by now. The concept terrified him, the single word echoing through his mind. Blind, blind, blind. But even that terror was overshadowed by his dread of death. He could feel it reaching out for him, taking him down to join the warriors beneath the soil, who had fought to defend this once great civilisation.

And then suddenly, miraculously, his vision returned, the grip on his throat relaxed, and he dropped to the ground. Raiza had released him. Thomas stared up at the boy he once knew. The burning green eyes had lost their flare, the twisted face eased into the complexion Thomas was familiar with.

"Run, Thomas..." Raiza croaked. "He would have killed you, he really would, but I couldn't let him..."

"What are you talking about?" Thomas gasped.

"The voice, the whispering voice. I can hold him back, but not for long. Run, Thomas!"

Thomas unsteadily got up. Whatever was happening to Raiza, it had given him an opportunity to escape. He turned, and began to limp away, still staring at his near-murderer.

"Faster, Thomas, faster! For God's sake, Thomas, run! I can't hold him for much longer, I can't-"

Raiza convulsed sharply, and his eyes rolled in their sockets. Thomas started to run.

"Foolish mortal," Raiza cried. *"You are in my grasp, now. Give in.* No! I've had enough! *You will give into my power.* Get out of my mind!"

Listening to the conversation, Thomas realised that whatever was left of the boy he had known was fighting back, battling against the entity that possessed his body. Thomas sped up, fleeing across the wasteland like a terrified rabbit.

"I will never leave you, mortal. Get away from me! *No... you are mine to do with-* Leave – *As* - Me – *I* – Alone – *wish!"*

Raiza convulsed again, and bile sprayed from his mouth as his body fought against itself. Still, though he was running at full speed, Thomas' head remained turned as he stared with both horror and intrigue at the unseen battle.

"My power cannot be broken. My will cannot be broken. You may be the Fall, mortal, but you cannot hope to defeat me. Get away, get away! *I've already told you, I cannot "get away." The day I leave you is the day you die."*

Thomas glanced ahead of him, momentarily turning from the spectacle. Impossibly, he had stumbled into a circle of stones – a monolith gate. Remembering Eve's words, he closed his eyes, and concentrated on the Atlantis gate. Behind him, he could still hear Raiza's fight with the entity possessing him.

"No! Get out of my mind! *Silence! My patience has ended! You belong to me!*"

Raiza screamed in pain, a searing light flashed across the monolith gate, and Thomas fell forward into nothing.

When Thomas woke, he found himself lying on a bed. It was wonderfully soft, and Thomas allowed himself to sink deeper into its embrace. Someone had must have undressed him, for he was wearing a loose white shirt, and similar white trousers. For a moment, he was blissfully at peace.

And then he remembered. Remembered Malcaractimus' death, Raiza's fight with himself, and how he had fled. How he had ran, ran and ran, and how he had reached the Monolith Gate. How he had travelled to Atlantis. How he had stumbled out of the portal into Ingar's arms. How the merman had carried him through the halls, and laid him on the bed. And how he had sunk into sleep.

Where was Nick? Terror gripped him as the crash replayed itself in his mind. How Malcaractimus had torn him from the ship, how the stricken vessel had been tossed away into the wind, and how it had smashed into pieces against the docking tower.

There was no way his friends could have survived.

And then a voice penetrated his thoughts. It was a soft, gentle voice, and yet it sent shivers down his spine. Eve's voice.

"You're awake," she observed. Thomas sat up. The mermaid was seated by the window, watching him. Her dress was a stunning blue, and it glittered like the scales of a fish. He opened his mouth, but Eve cut him off.

"Ingar was worried about you. He thought it would be best if someone kept an eye on you in the night."

"But," Thomas stuttered. "I thought you were... the ship..."

"Oh, it crashed. To be honest, I thought we were dead. But then, there was this light..." she trailed off.

"Go on," Thomas prompted.

Eve was silent for a moment. She stood up, and sat on the edge of Thomas' bed. When she spoke, her voice seemed distant. "It was this yellow glow. Warm and inviting. It shone through the ship. It was so bright... but then through the light... I could barely make it out. But it was a tree. At least I think so. I don't know how it was on the ship, but I saw it. And there was a voice: "Eve," it said. It knew my name. "Eve, daughter of the sea. Your time in this universe has not yet expired. You have a greater purpose yet." And then..."

She fumbled in a pocket, and produced what seemed like a vial of blue water. Not normal water, not the clear blue liquid humans drink. No, it was actually blue, bright, shining blue. Blue like the sky, and blue like the sea.

"This appeared in my hands. The voice said something about it. "These are the tears of Celestria," it said. "When all seems lost, let them restore." And then I was here, in Atlantis."

Thomas stared at her. "Wow..." he breathed. "Do you think that voice was what saved me? When I was running, I found a monolith gate, right where I needed it to be. The chance was so small, but perhaps..."

And then a thought struck him. "The others," he said. "Did they survive too?"

Eve's face whitened. "Alex did. He's here in the building."

"And Nick?"

Eve shook her head, and burst into tears. Thomas put his arms around her, and she buried her face in his shoulder, her tears soaking into his shirt. Thomas had no idea how long they sat there like that, Eve weeping, Thomas just holding her, the occasional soft word of comfort penetrating the silence.

Nick had always been the strongest of them. He had always known what was going on. He was always the one with the answer, he always solved the problems. And now he was gone. Why? How? How could Eve and Alex have been saved by some strange light, but Nick left behind?

Thomas tried to speak, but the words caught in his throat, and he found himself crying as well. What hope did they have without Nick?

After a few minutes, there was a soft knock on the door. Ingar pushed it open. "Come," he said. "If you are recovered, His Grace Prometheus will address you."

Prometheus was not well, that much was certain. His normal composure seemed off balance, somehow. His perfect face was creased, as if with age, and his eyes had sunk deeper into their sockets, dark shadows forming beneath them. Seeing Thomas, he brightened a little, and smiled.

"Thomas Colfrey," he said. "Quite the hero of the hour, so I hear."

Thomas smiled back. "I don't really think so, sir. I nearly got myself killed."

"Quite," the king replied. "But, I must remark, you are the very first being in the universe to escape from Mal... Mal..." He frowned. "I can barely remember his name. Others have noticed it too. Any thoughts of the... demons have been dimmed, and the monsters themselves are gone. Even the Throne of Bones sits empty, though I know whoever did this will arise to fill it. I sense some great sorcery at work, and it fills me with dread."

"I think I can help with that," Thomas replied. "Raiza cast some sort of spell, he-"

"Raiza?" Prometheus asked, raising an eyebrow. Ingar stepped out of the shadows. "The other human boy I told you about, Your Grace," he said. "The boy whose body isn't quite his own."

"Ah," said the king. "But what was he doing there?"

Thomas shuffled uneasily. "I think I'd better start at the beginning, sir," he said, and for the second time since he arrived in Mythicia, Thomas launched into his tale.

Epilogue

The Calling

Lokar snorted, and hurled his opponent to the floor. It was his sixth victory in the ring that morning, and the Bull-King was clearly impressed. Here in the Minotaur Kingdom, victory meant the King's favour, and the King's favour meant wealth. The tournament referee trotted across the ring, and handed Lokar a small black coin.

It was a Victory Coin. With ten Victory Coins, a fighter could enter the finals, and stand a chance of winning the million drisk prize. He took the coin from the minotaur, and strode out of the ring.

He stepped out of the arena, and strolled along the dirt track linking the amphitheatre to the residential areas. It was as he salvaged his communicator from a well-worn pocket, that he heard... the Calling. It was impossible to explain, but he felt like he was somehow being pulled away, across the world. He thought he heard a strange voice, whispering quietly in his head, as if spoken from a great distance.

"Meot ceom, llawthing sild. Meot ceom."

Lokar twitched. He suddenly felt the desire to walk, to walk away, and to go to... Odmehlwor. Yes, that was where he had to go. To Odmehlwor. The question of why didn't matter, he just... had to.

The minotaur drew himself up, headed to the local docking station, and boarded a ship for Odmehlwor.

Lithwaster the hydra twisted in her sleep. She was dreaming of the sea, her long lost home, where she knew she belonged. And yet she could not go there. Not now. Not when the demons held her here, a captive sealed away in an inescapable cell, all but forgotten until she was summoned to battle. She hadn't always been alone in this hellish prison. There had been others of her race, of course there had. But when the warden came for them, they never returned.

She awoke, and stared at the cold, black stone of the walls that trapped her here. Here, on the demonic wastes of Arach'barba. She groaned, wallowing in her unparalleled misery.

And then she heard... the Calling. It was impossible to explain, but she felt like she was somehow being pulled away, across the world. She thought she heard a strange voice, whispering quietly in her heads, as if spoken from a great distance.

"Mȩot cȩom, llawthing sild. Mȩot cȩom."

Lithwaster twitched. She suddenly felt the desire to walk, to walk away, and to go to... Odmehlwor. Yes, that was where she had to go. To Odmehlwor. The question of why didn't matter, she just... had to.

With a mighty roar, she hurled herself against the black walls that imprisoned her. Weakened by some hidden power, they shattered, and she charged across the blackened plains, to find a ship.

When Nicholas the Wise opened his eyes, the first thing he knew was pain. Pain, pain, overwhelming his senses, destroying his mind. He felt unconsciousness begin to tug at him again. He shook it off, stood up, and immediately regretted it. He must have broken his leg in at least three different places. It certainly hurt like hell.

He collapsed back into the rubble, and closed his eyes. Everything hurt. Where was he? Was he dead? That must be it. There was no way he could have survived the crash. The crash! He remembered now. The flames, the explosions, Malcaractimus, and then - nothing. Well, if this was Heaven, it certainly wasn't everything it was made out to be. He must've just been knocked unconscious, but what now? He could barely stand, let alone walk. Let alone get off this planet. He was doomed, doomed to die in these ruins, forgotten. Alone.

The others probably thought he was dead. Alex and Eve, they were on the ship too. They must have been killed. He had had his magic to protect him, and still he hadn't the strength to get up.

And what about Thomas? Malcaractimus would no doubt have killed him – the boy hadn't had nearly enough time to prepare for fighting the Emperor. But then again, there was always his Bloodrage. Perhaps, just perhaps it could have been enough for him to get away. But no, he couldn't count on that. The likelihood was that Mythicia's last hope was dead, and there was nothing he had left to live for. He closed his eyes.

"Nicholas the Wise..." a voice whispered.

Another bolt of pain ripped through him, the voice bringing its own sensations of fear and recognition. It could only belong to Raiza. Was Raiza even the right word? Nick dimly remembered the boy from his time on Earth, and the entity that he had now become was so much more hideously twisted than anything else he had ever encountered. It wasn't Raiza anymore. Nick snapped open his eyes, and stared up at the figure. "Can't you just leave an old man to die?" he moaned, sounding braver than he felt.

"I could indeed..." Raiza replied, a ghost of a smile dancing across his lips. The green eyes narrowed, shining ever the brighter. *"But that is*

not your fate. Destiny holds more in store for you yet, mage."

"What do you want with me?" Nick asked bluntly. He had nothing to lose – gods knew he was nearing the end anyway. There wasn't any point beating about the bush.

"*Want...*" Raiza paused, wrapping the word around his tongue as if savouring its flavour. *"I want nothing with you. At least, not in your present state..."*

Nick frowned, uncomprehending. The creature was talking in riddles. What the hell did it matter what the damn thing meant anyway? "Leave me alone."

"No..." Raiza grinned sadistically, his eyes glittering in the twilight. *"You are far too valuable for me to leave to die... Mẹot cẹom, llawthing sild. Mẹot cẹom."*

And Nicholas the Wise heard the Calling.

A Note From the Author

Hi, it's me, Joseph Russell, but of course you know that from reading the cover page. Unless you didn't, in which case have a look now. See it there? That's my name, under "The Mythicia Chronicles," which incidentally is pronounced "Mith-Iss-Ee-Uh." In future, pay more attention to the cover of a book.

Anyway, now that's nice and clear, let's move on to what I actually want to say, which I'm sure will come to me in a moment. Until then, I'll just keep waffling on and on like this. Right. I've added in this note at the end to say thanks to everyone who needs thanking.

To begin with, I'd like to thank my parents, for helping me through the writing of this book. Without them, it'd never have happened. Well, without them, I'd never have been born, but that's just being pedantic.

Next, I think I'll thank my brother. I'm not quite sure what I'm thanking him for, but thanks all the same.

I can hardly go without thanking Kaan Vardal for the truly spectacular front cover art he drew for me. He's only a few months older than me and did a fantastic job in the time I gave him.

Now, onto the tricky bits. I think I'll thank my various English teachers, who have had the misfortune to be piled with various versions and re-writes of the book, and also for helping to teach me English, but most of the credit for that goes to my parents and brother.

I'd also like to thank my class, which changed towards the end of the book. So thanks to 2YZ and 3AMM.

And thanks (or not) to the annoying little year 7s and 8s who plagued my very existence as soon as they discovered my writings, and will probably still plague me for years to come. You know who you are.

I'd also like to thank two people without whom my dream of Mythicia would perhaps not yet have been realised. Their names are Andrew Baker and Alan Durant. Andrew is the lawyer who has kept the rights to Mythicia safe for me, and Alan was the first man to read and review my novel, pointing out the good, the bad and the ugly of it and sending me off in the right direction.

And as I come to the end of this note, I mustn't forget to thank Skitty and Stormageddon-Destroyer-of-Worlds, the two chickens who weren't even hatched when I started the Mythicia Chronicles, but are now a fundamental part of the family.

And of course, thanks to you.

Joseph Russell, 18 August 2011

Printed in Great Britain
by Amazon.co.uk, Ltd.,
Marston Gate.